VAMPIRE'S KISS

VAMPIRE'S KISS

Legion of Angels: Book 1

www.ellasummers.com/vampires-kiss

ISBN 978-1-5396-3503-1

Copyright © 2016 by Ella Summers

All rights reserved.

VAMPIRE'S KISS
Legion of Angels: Book 1

Ella Summers

Books by Ella Summers

Legion of Angels
1   Vampire's Kiss
2   Witch's Cauldron

Dragon Born Shadow World
The Complete Trilogy

Dragon Born Serafina
1   Mercenary Magic
2   Magic Games
3   Magic Nights
4   Rival Magic

Dragon Born Alexandria
1   Magic Edge
2   Blood Magic
3   Magic Kingdom
4   Shadow Magic [2017]

Dragon Born Awakening
1   Fairy Magic
2   Spirit Magic [2017]

More Books by Ella Summers

Sorcery and Science Collections
    1   The Land of Magic
    2   The Mad Prophet
    3   War of Empires [2017]

Read more at
www.ellasummers.com

Chapters

PROLOGUE
Prologue / 1

CHAPTER ONE
Purgatory / 2

CHAPTER TWO
Pandora's Box / 13

CHAPTER THREE
Gods and Demons / 30

CHAPTER FOUR
Ghosts / 40

CHAPTER FIVE
The Legion of Angels / 45

CHAPTER SIX
The Last Day of My Life / 66

CHAPTER SEVEN
First Sip / 81

CHAPTER EIGHT
What Doesn't Kill You... / 88

CHAPTER NINE
The Torturer of Desperate Souls / 95

CHAPTER TEN
Firefall / 110

CHAPTER ELEVEN
Vampire's Kiss / 119

CHAPTER TWELVE
Back to Purgatory / 127

CHAPTER THIRTEEN
The Black Plains / 140

CHAPTER FOURTEEN
Heaven / 153

CHAPTER FIFTEEN
The Wicked Wilds / 170

CHAPTER SIXTEEN
The Next Generation of Monsters / 180

CHAPTER SEVENTEEN
Perfect Balance / 187

CHAPTER EIGHTEEN
Sweet Dreams / 195

CHAPTER NINETEEN
Steel and Bones / 203

CHAPTER TWENTY
Magic in a Bottle / 210

CHAPTER TWENTY-ONE
Secret / 215

CHAPTER TWENTY-TWO
The Promise / 220

Prologue

NO ONE KNEW why the monsters came, and no one saw them coming. Within days, they had all but overrun the Earth.

Some people said it was humanity's punishment for its sins. Others said it was the demons who'd unleashed the beasts on us. But one thing we know for sure: powerful beings stepped in. They called themselves gods, and they stood against the monsters.

They built walls between Earth's remaining cities and the plains of beasts. They gave us food and weapons—but most of all, they gave us magic.

From the survivors of humanity, they built their army, soldiers with the magic of vampires, witches, shifters, fairies, and all kinds of other supernatural beings. And the best of the best, the top of their Legion, they made into angels. With this new army, the gods won the war against the demons, pushing them back into hell.

The monster problem, however, was not so easily fixed. The beasts remained. Two hundred years later, the battle still rages on Earth, but piece by piece, we are going to take back our world.

CHAPTER ONE
Purgatory

YOU KNEW YOUR life had hit a new low when your sixty-year-old inebriated next-door neighbor offered you a 'quickie' behind the bar of the Witch's Watering Hole. I was still thinking up a diplomatic response when he plunked down a glass jar of cloudy alcohol to sweeten the deal.

"What do you say, Leda?" he slurred, smacking his lips. His breath smelled like acetone.

That you're three times my age. I reminded myself that he was drunk—and that it wasn't nice to throw your drink in your neighbor's face.

He wasn't the only one. The Witch's Watering Hole was packed tonight, an inevitable consequence of payday and Friday night colliding. Everyone in the bar was drunk—everyone, that was, except for me. I had work to do and no time for moonshine.

"Dale," I said, smiling. Yes, he was drunk, but that was no reason to forget my manners. "I'm flattered. Really I am, but I think Cindy would be very disappointed if I took you up on your offer." I gave the busty redhead across the room a little wave.

Dale followed my gaze to Cindy. As soon as his eyes fell

upon her, her full lips spread into a sultry smile and she shifted in her seat, crossing one very long leg over the other with leisurely ease. Her miniskirt slid a few inches up her thigh, which sealed the deal for Dale. He stumbled off his barstool and staggered toward her, puffing out his chest like a peacock.

I slid the jar of abandoned moonshine to a safe distance, then took a sip of my pineapple juice to cleanse my senses. Despite his questionable taste in alcohol—which, to be fair, half the town was also drinking—Dale wasn't actually a bad guy. He was usually very quiet and friendly. He'd probably regret his lewd words in the morning. Assuming he even remembered them.

The shiny red jukebox in the corner blared to life, singing out a humorous song about a witch who'd fallen for a vampire. The jukebox was a recent import from New York City, and Brooke, the owner of the Witch's Watering Hole, was quite proud of it. As well she should be. This bar was the only one in town that had a jukebox.

Out here on the Frontier, at the dividing line between civilization and the monster-infested Wasteland, we didn't have a lot of amenities. It was no wonder that the survivors of the Scourge had renamed this town Purgatory.

Besides the jukebox, the rest of the Witch's Watering Hole looked like the quintessential old western saloon, which was probably the era the furnishings had come out of. Handmade wood tables and chairs, rundown but clean, sat at the edges of the room, leaving a small dancing area beside the jukebox.

Overhead, an old fan turned slowly, stirring the thick summer air. Most things here were powered by good old water or mundane steam, and the fan was no exception. The jukebox, however, was of a whole other class. Its power source was enchanted steam—or Magitech—an energy the gods had gifted humanity two centuries ago. Well, at least if you happened to be lucky enough to live in one of the world's high-tech cities. For everyone else, the enchanted energy was difficult—if not impossible—to get. And it was *always* egregiously expensive.

"You look nice tonight, Leda."

I turned around to face my next admirer. That was the sixth guy so far tonight. Maybe the crop top and hot pants hadn't been the best wardrobe idea after all. But I had to attract my mark's attention somehow. If only he'd gotten here an hour ago like Calli's intelligence had said he would, then I'd be long gone by now.

Admirer #6 turned out to be Jak, the shy nerdy kid who'd had a crush on me since third grade—and yet had never spoken more than three words to me. Until tonight. Tonight, the words were gushing out.

"So, do you want…um, what I mean is…only if you'd like to…"

His hand held to the jar of moonshine for dear life. So that's where his sudden burst of courage had come from. He'd swiped Dale's glass from the counter. Finder's Keepers was the motto out here, and most people just accepted it. Besides, Dale was too busy making out with his new friend to notice his missing moonshine.

"…I was thinking it might be nice to…you know, seeing how long we've known each other…"

"Spit it out, Jak," I said, checking the impatience in my voice. It wasn't his fault that my mark was late or that five other men had hit on me before he'd wandered over.

"Dance with me?" he blurted out. He was squeezing the jar's handle so hard that all color had drained from his hand.

"Take a hike, junior," someone said behind Jak, causing him to jump.

Jak took one look at the cold gleam in the man's dark eyes, then ran off. The new arrival gave the moonshine a disgusted look, then ordered a whiskey.

"I'm Mark," the man said, extending his hand. He smelled strongly of cologne and peppermint.

He was as out of place in this bar as the shiny red jukebox in the corner. The bar's other patrons wore faded cotton and denim. They had smudged faces and dirt under their fingernails. Mark looked like he'd stepped off a fashion runway. He wore a black silk shirt, half of the buttons undone to expose his muscular chest. Boots with a slight heel over form-fitting black leather pants completed his ensemble. His hair was combed back and styled with gel. Platinum blond, it was nearly as pale as my own. Except his hair was dyed, clearly an expensive color job from a high-end city salon.

"Leda," I replied, smiling demurely at my mark. I'd have been able to peg him even without having seen the photograph on his wanted poster. He stood out like a sore thumb. And the irony of my mark's name being Mark was hard to ignore.

"Leda," he said, as though he were savoring every letter of my name. "Such a beautiful name." He looked over his glass, returning the smile. "For such a beautiful woman."

Smooth. Real smooth. He spoke with an easy grace, as though he didn't have a care in the world. As though he weren't on the run from the law.

"You're not from around here," I said, trailing my gaze down the length of him as though I were checking him out. He wasn't wearing any weapons that I could see.

"I'm from the city. New York," he added with a

conspiring wink.

"Oh," I gasped. "I've always wanted to go there." I fluttered my long eyelashes at him.

He took the bait. "Maybe I'll take you sometime," he said, wrapping his arm around me.

I moved in closer, reaching around him to run my hands down his back. No weapons. I moved down to his legs. Nothing. Either he was very good at concealing them, or he was an idiot. I was leaning toward idiot. After all, he *had* given me his real name. He seemed to think he was safe out here on the border of civilization.

"Would you really take me?" I asked.

"Of course, honey."

Liar. He was on the run from the New York authorities, charged with kidnapping *and* theft of Legion property. The only way he'd be going back to the city was in handcuffs. Preferably mine.

"You smell so good," he muttered into my ear. "Has anyone ever told you that?"

Only every other guy who wanted into my pants.

I kissed his smooth jaw, then pulled back to hit him with my best sultry look. Despite hours of practice in front of the mirror, I still didn't have the best bedroom eyes, but Mark didn't seem to care. He leered at me as I stirred my pineapple juice with one hand. The other hand was busy discreetly dipping into my purse for the handcuffs…

"Hello, Leda!" a voice belted from across the bar.

I knew that voice all too well. I glared at the bounty hunter coming my way. He wore a black-and-red leather motorcycle suit that was a hundred times cooler than he was. Jinx. That's what he called himself, and I didn't know his real name. Only that he was a scavenger. A damn hyena.

"Hey, sweetie pie." Jinx stopped in front of me,

grinning.

"Do you know this fellow?" Mark asked.

"Unfortunately," I growled.

"Leda and I go way back," Jinx said. "We met during the Sunset job."

Shut up. I tried mentally sending him that message on all frequencies, but I'm not a telepath, so my message fell on deaf ears.

"Or was it the Blacktown affair? I can't for the life of me remember which." He laughed. "We've done so many jobs together."

No, you've stolen many jobs from me, you thieving son of a bitch.

"What kind of business are you two in?" Mark asked.

"Bounty hunting," Jinx replied pleasantly. "Speaking of which, Leda, did you ever catch that guy out of New York?"

Stools tumbled, scraping against the floor as Mark bolted for the door, running out of the bar like his tail was on fire. I glared at Jinx, but there was no time to tell him off—and I wasn't strong enough to best him in hand-to-hand combat. But I was fast. I had him handcuffed to the bar before he could move, then I dashed out after my mark, Jinx's stream of enraged curses bouncing off my heels.

Now out on the open street, I pumped my legs as fast as I could. My boots barely touched the gravelly ground. I had to get to Mark before he escaped—or worse yet, Jinx got him. The cuffs wouldn't hold the other bounty hunter for long.

"Leda, our mark just turned down Third Street. I'm in pursuit," my brother Zane said over the comms. The tiny Magitech-powered device hidden inside my earring had cost us a small fortune, but it was worth every penny. It made teamwork like this possible.

"Keep your eyes peeled for Jinx," I told him.

I was *not* letting that scavenger muscle in on our gig—not this time. We couldn't afford to lose this paycheck. We'd already spent the money to pay our sister Bella's first tuition bill to the New York University of Witchcraft.

"Shit."

"Zane?" I asked.

"Mark is headed for the wall."

If he made it over the wall, we'd lose any chance at that bounty. I ignored the raging hellfire burning inside my muscles and pushed my protesting body to move faster as I sprinted around the corner onto Third Street. Now, I was a fast runner. It was an essential skill for someone always chasing people. I practiced hard and long every day, and as a result, I could outrun almost anyone.

But not Mark. He moved *fast*, especially for someone wearing unbroken leather pants.

The wall stood tall and imposing at the end of the street. Beyond it lay the Wasteland, where monsters roamed freely, uncontrolled, unchecked, unstoppable. That wall was all that stood between this town and an all-out slaughter—that wall and the paranormal soldiers who stood guard atop it. The soldiers watched Mark run toward the wall, and they didn't even lift their rifles. Their job was to keep the monsters out. If someone wanted to run off into the Wasteland, they wouldn't lift a finger to stop him, criminal or not. They knew the monsters would get him anyway, and they got paid either way.

We, on the other hand, only got paid if we brought Mark in alive. Which wouldn't happen if he ran off into the Wasteland. Maybe we could get him before the monsters did, but I wasn't about to risk our lives out there. I might be crazy, but I'm not *that* crazy. Not like some other bounty hunters.

Mark jumped into the air, hitting the wall. He was going to climb it. The wall was over thirty feet tall, and he thought he could tackle it with just his bare hands.

Maybe he was right. He was making surprisingly fast progress. Too fast. We'd never be able to overtake him.

I was still too far away. So I pulled out my gun and shot him in the leg. Mark howled, his cry piercing the crickets' evening song. When he didn't let go of the wall, I shot him again—this time in the hand. His grip slipped, and he slid down the stony surface. As soon as his feet hit the ground, he spun around to glare at Zane, his eyes pulsing with a distinctive silver-blue sheen.

"A vampire," Zane gasped inside my earpiece.

Well, that explained his speed.

"His file said he was human," I said, running toward them.

"Guess it was wrong."

Fantastic. Mark darted forward, backhanding Zane across the street. My brother hit the ground hard. I lifted my gun to shoot the vampire again, but he was in front of me in an instant. Growling, he knocked the weapon from my hand, then slammed me against the wall.

I kicked and pushed against his iron grip, but he didn't give an inch. This was why I didn't fight people up close, especially not vampires. Thanks to my mystery supernatural blood—no one seemed to know what kind of supernatural I was supposed to be—I'm stronger and more resilient than a human. Otherwise, I'd have already been dead. But I was not stronger than a vampire. That was undeniably obvious as Mark's hand closed around my throat, his tightening grip slowly choking the air out of my lungs.

Then he just let go. His body fell away, revealing Zane

standing behind him with a taser. The vampire snarled and smacked him to the ground.

Still coughing out bruised breaths, I pivoted around, looking for something—anything—that could help me against a vampire. I came up short. Paranormal soldiers had potions and guns with magic bullets to help them fight the supernatural baddies. My options were more limited. I grabbed a steel rod off the wall, bracing my legs to free it. As the vampire turned away from Zane to face me, I swung the rod at his head. The force of the impact knocked him to the ground.

He jumped up, enraged, but I was already moving, running toward my gun. I snatched it off the ground and unloaded everything I had into him. If I'd known that I'd be facing a vampire tonight, I would have brought along something more potent than these weak tranquilizers. I wasn't even sure they did anything to vampires—well, except annoy them.

The bullets did slow him down, but not enough. He rushed toward me, murder shining in his eyes. I avoided the first punch—but not the second. I was too slow. As I turned, his fist grazed my ribs, brushing them. If I'd been a fraction of a second slower, his blow would have broken them. His next punch took me hard in the head. My head spinning, my vision clouded, I tripped to the ground.

I scrambled to my feet, but his hand closed around my leg, holding me down. Scratching furiously at the ground, I scooped up two handfuls of dry dirt and hurled them into those inhuman silver-blue eyes. His hands flew to his face, trying to rub the dust away. I jumped up, ignoring the fresh surge of pain in my side. There would be time to be wounded later—when an enraged vampire wasn't trying to kill me.

I snatched an old sweater from a nearby clothes line, wrapping it around the biggest rock I could find. Then I swung it at the vampire's head. He roared, falling back. But before I could hit him again, he jumped up, pushing me and my rock to the ground. He kicked a fresh helping of pain into my side. Then he stared down at me, wiping the blood from his mouth.

"You shouldn't have come after me," he said, lifting his boot over my head.

Pain and shock twisted together inside of my stomach. I grabbed his leg, trying to shove his boot off my face.

"It's a shame really," he said, his boot pushing harder, overpowering my feeble attempts to free myself. "You're such a pretty girl. I hate to stomp your skull in." He smiled wistfully. "But I really must."

I pushed and kicked and punched with every shred of strength in me. And it didn't make a damn difference. He angled his foot for a killing blow.

And then he just stopped.

Zane came up behind him, chanting under his breath. The vampire staggered back, holding his head, roaring in agony.

"Stop," Mark growled, his voice cracking. He dropped to his knees.

But Zane didn't stop. He continued his telepathic assault. The vampire roared and raged, his wild movements knocking Zane over. Fury flooded me, displacing pain, filling me with strength. I leapt to my feet and tore an old shutter off of a nearby building. Adrenaline soaring, I swung it at the vampire, hammering it straight through his abdomen. Shock sparked in his eyes, then he passed out.

I limped over to Zane, my crashing adrenaline letting the pain back in. "Are you all right?" I asked as I helped my brother to his feet.

"Fine." He looked from the vampire to me. "What the hell was that, Leda?"

"I got mad."

His eyes widened. "I can see that."

"Ok, enough fun," I said. "Let's get this vampire tied up and brought in before he decides to wake up."

CHAPTER TWO
Pandora's Box

"THIS IS A vampire," I said as Zane and I dumped the sleeping vampire onto the sofa of Sheriff Wilder's reception lounge. The window shutter lodged in Mark's gut shifted, and a fresh gush of blood sprinkled across the sofa's faded green fabric.

The sheriff's eighteen-year-old daughter was already at the phone, buzzing her father's line. She was the office secretary. I'd met her a bunch of times coming into the sheriff's office after a job. She'd always been so bubbly, so vibrant. I'd never seen her freak out like this. Then again, I'd never brought in a bleeding vampire on her shift. They weren't exactly the teddy bears of the paranormal world—well, unless you got all warm and fuzzy about having your neck chewed on. Honestly, I'd never understood the appeal.

"He wasn't supposed to be a vampire," I continued.

Carmen Wilder's eyes darted back and forth from the vampire drooling on their sofa to the blinking telephone. She mashed the button a few more times.

"Nothing in his file even hinted that he was a vampire. The file *you* gave me said he was human," I finished as the sheriff himself, Leland Wilder, rushed into the reception lounge.

"It must have been a new development," he said, his face going as pale as his whitewashed walls.

"You knew." I glared at him. "You knew, and you didn't say anything."

"I didn't," he insisted, leaning down to throw the vampire over his shoulder. Leland Wilder might have been well over fifty, but he was no slouch. He was built like a warhorse. "Really, Leda. I had no idea."

Metal screeched as he opened the cell door. He tossed the vampire inside, then turned the lock. A golden glow—like a million buzzing fireflies—spread across the bars. The sheriff's office was one of the few places in town powered by Magitech. The gigantic wall that stood between Purgatory and the Wasteland was the notable other. With the flip of a switch, the soldiers guarding the wall could power up the magic generator, and a protective shield would flare to life. They hadn't had to do it yet—so far, the monsters were keeping their distance from the town—but you never knew when they'd decide their big slice of hell just wasn't big enough.

"Bringing in this vampire nearly killed us," I told him.

"I'm sorry."

"I don't want apologies. I want answers."

He lifted his hand, waving me into his office. I followed him inside, not waiting for Zane. He was busy comforting Carmen. She'd already nearly forgotten about the bleeding vampire sleeping in the jail cell. My brother, the charmer.

Sheriff Wilder closed the door behind me, then sat down on the edge of his desk. "Do you want some tea? Coffee?" His gaze dipped to my blood-smeared bare midriff. "A healing potion?"

I folded my arms across my chest. "Just answers. What's

going on here?"

"I wish I knew." He sighed. "The paranormal police precinct that issued the bounty didn't tell me Mark Silverstream is a vampire. I just called it in to get a pickup and gave them a piece of my mind about keeping this from me."

"And what did they say?"

"That Silverstream was turned after he escaped custody in New York," the sheriff replied. "He must have called in a favor, maybe got someone to turn him outside the system."

"And the paranormal police didn't put it on the poster because then they'd have to pay more for the reward."

"It's not just about the money, Leda. Lately, bounty hunters have been wary about tracking down vampires. I don't blame them, especially after what happened in Brimstone."

Vampires had a very strict hierarchy and tomes of rules. Rules about who got to be turned. About where they could live. About who and how they could fight. About how they may speak and who they could eat. It was all very medieval, but it was these rules that kept the vampires—and their bloody instincts—in check.

But a few months ago, a group of vampires went rogue. They took over a small town called Brimstone, claiming it as their own. By the time the bounty hunters arrived on the scene, the vampires had already killed half the humans in town. The bounty hunters soon followed them to their graves.

The paranormal soldiers went in next. They managed to take out a few of the vampires before they were discovered, but as soon as they were, it was game over. The vampires massacred them. None of them made it out alive.

Finally, the Legion was sent in. The Legion of Angels

were the elite supernatural soldiers, their powers gifted to them by the gods themselves. They were the ones called in when things went really bad—like apocalyptic bad. They upheld the gods' order. They dealt out punishment without hesitation or mercy. If the Legion sent their soldiers to kill you, you were already dead. They were deadly efficient, and more powerful than anyone on Earth.

At the head of the Legion were the angels. And you did *not* want to get on their bad side. They were as brutal as they were beautiful, all shining white halo and everything.

The Legion had declared what happened at Brimstone an 'incident'. Everyone else called it an all-out catastrophe. Of course bounty hunters were feeling skittish nowadays about going after vampires. I wouldn't have taken the job either if I'd known the mark was one of them.

"The paranormal police can play dumb all they want, but the fact remains that something like this doesn't just fall through the cracks," I told the sheriff. "They knew. They must have."

He didn't say anything. He looked like he didn't know what to say. Leland Wilder was a honest man, and the idea of anyone in his hierarchy lying just didn't process. It overloaded his sense of justice.

So maybe I'd just have to kick him toward reality. "Lying to a bounty hunter about a fugitive's supernatural status is against regulations," I reminded him. "We were armed for a human, not a vampire. I nearly died tonight. My *brother* nearly died. I'm not letting this go. We'll be filing a complaint with the government."

"I wish I could too," he muttered, so quietly that I wasn't sure if I'd heard him right.

I didn't comment on it anyway. This town's sheriff's office was severely understaffed and underfunded. The

Magitech generator that powered their jail cells was their only indulgence—and there had been rumors that the government would be taking it away too. Magic wasn't cheap. There were hundreds of Frontier towns screaming for upgrades, and not enough money to go around. I didn't even want to think about how much it cost to maintain the wall. It stretched on for thousands of miles.

The self-professed district 'lords' here in Purgatory and other Frontier towns had offered to help with the funding problem, but that would just be trading one problem for another. The district lords were criminals themselves. In fact, the crime lords were already as big of a problem as the underfunded sheriff's office. And once word got out about the job tonight—and bounty hunters learned that they couldn't trust the information in their marks' files anymore—the problem would only get worse.

"Leda, please don't tell the other bounty hunters what happened tonight."

"They have a right to know, Sheriff. They put their lives on the line every time they take a job."

"I know. But this is just the thing the district lords were waiting for, their chance to move in. If bounty hunters stop taking jobs here, I'll have to take the lords' help. I don't have to tell you what that will do to this town."

Maybe the district lords had been behind this whole thing. Maybe they'd been the ones to make sure no one found out about Mark—until it was too late. It was exactly the sort of game they'd play. And if Zane and I had died, there would have been no containing this incident. Oh, the joys of being a pawn in someone else's power play!

"It's not up to me," I told him. "It's up to Calli to share or not share. But even if she decides not to tell people, it will eventually get out, you know."

The sheriff sighed. "I know. I'll have to think of something. Somehow." He rubbed his head like life hurt. "Your payment is being transferred to the usual account."

"Thanks."

I opened the door and stepped out into the reception lounge. Zane and Carmen were sitting side-by-side on the edge of the desk, the vampire in the jail cell completely forgotten. It was amazing what a little flirting could cure. I waited while Zane lifted Carmen's hand to his lips and softly kissed her fingertips. She giggled, giving him a little wave as we left the building. Like most young women, Carmen Wilder was not immune to my brother's charms.

"Come on, Casanova," I said, linking my arm in his. "Fighting vampires makes me hungry. Let's get home for dinner before our dear sisters leave nothing left for us."

◆ ◇ ◆ ◇ ◆

We made it home without incident, well except for the Pilgrims who swarmed us on the corner of Chastity and Fifth. They trailed us for six blocks, waxing poetic about the gods' divine message. They peppered their prose with copious quotes from the Book of the Gods, singing tales of how the gods had come to Earth to purge the land of monsters.

"If the gods are so powerful and the monsters have all been purged, then what are those things prowling around on the other side of that thirty-foot fence?" I couldn't help but ask them.

The Pilgrims expressed their outrage at my impertinent remark—then wandered off to find someone else's soul to save. By then, we were nearly home, and the cornucopia of delicious scents wafting out of the kitchen window drew us the rest of the way there.

Like most homes in Purgatory, our house was a modest one-story affair with four small bedrooms. I shared a bedroom with my sister Bella, while my other sisters Tessa and Gin shared theirs. Zane had his own room, a benefit of being the only man in the house. We called him the 'Wild Card' of Pandora's Box, the family bounty-hunting business. Calli, our mom, ran the business, and we all helped out.

None of us were blood relatives, though we were all of supernatural blood. That didn't mean we had any special powers, though. In fact, besides Bella and Zane, none of us did. Magic manifested differently in every person. Bella was a witch, Zane a telepath, and the rest of us were just a bit tougher and a little faster than normal humans. That was a huge asset in our line of work. Sometimes that extra edge meant the difference between catching your mark and watching it slip through your fingers.

Calli was the one who held us all together. She'd rescued our younger selves, taken us in when we'd had no one. I'd known only one mother before her, and she wasn't my blood relative either. Her name was Yasmine, and she'd been killed in a monster attack when I was ten. After her death, I'd lived on the streets for a few years—until Calli had found me and taken me in.

"Who's holed up in the bathroom this time?" Zane asked as we walked into the living room.

Our house had six people but only one bathroom. And if that wasn't bad enough, two of those people were seventeen-year-old girls.

Bella looked up from the dining room table she was setting for dinner, her strawberry-blonde locks tumbling over her shoulders. "I think Tessa is in there."

"Still?" I said. "She was in there earlier tonight, right when I needed to get ready for the job. I had to use the mirror of Calli's motorcycle to apply my makeup."

"Which is smudged." Bella brushed her thumb across my cheek. "What happened out there?"

Zane plopped down on the sofa. "Our mark was a vampire is what happened."

"Oh." Bella paled. "Zane, you know what Calli says about getting blood on the sofa."

"What can I say? I'm a rebel." He grinned at her.

In addition to his telepathic magic, Zane had other powers, the greatest of which was his uncanny ability to charm anyone. He was very popular with the ladies of this town. Young or old, they all fawned over him. He had an angelic face, one that you knew could do no wrong—even when he was doing wrong right in front of you.

"Rules are rules, whether for rebels or princes," Bella told him. Like the rest of the family, she was immune to his charms.

Zane shrugged. "It's leather. Blood washes right off. That's why we bought this sofa."

"Weren't you asking about the bathroom?" I reminded him. "I just saw Tessa leave. You might want to hurry and get in before she decides to try out a new lipstick."

Zane jumped up. "Good point. I need to shower."

"Hot date?" I teased.

"As a matter of fact, yes."

"Wait," Bella said as he turned to leave. She set a small glass bottle into his hand. "Drink this. It will heal your injuries."

"Thanks," he said, beaming at her.

Laughing under her breath, she shooed him away with a lace handkerchief, the perfect complement to the lacy white dress she was wearing tonight. Then she wiped down the sofa where he'd been sitting.

"You should drink one too," Bella said, tossing me a potion bottle when she was done fluffing up the pillows. She just couldn't help herself. My sister was a complete neat freak.

I popped the cap and chugged it down in one go. Mmm, strawberries. Bella made the best healing potions. The standard apothecary ones tasted like old shoelaces.

"I'd better report in to the boss," I told her.

"Good luck."

I brushed down my wrinkled top, then marched into the kitchen. The smell was even better inside, at the core of Calli's culinary genius, than it had been outside. Calli stood with her back to me, stirring and seasoning the various dishes cooking on the stove. I swiped a breadstick from the basket on the counter.

"You smell like blood," Calli said without even turning. I swear, that woman must have been a bloodhound in a former life.

"That's what happens when our mark turns out to be a vampire."

Calli turned, her dark brows scrunching together as she looked me up and down. "You should have Bella look at your wounds."

I took a bite out of my breadstick, savoring the taste of garlic butter melting into my tongue. "Already done. She gave me a potion."

Bella was our team's witch. She made all of our healing potions and magic bombs, which was much cheaper than buying them. Unfortunately, that's exactly what we'd have to do soon. She'd been accepted into the New York University of Witchcraft, and she was leaving tomorrow.

"Have you found someone to take over as team witch?" I asked Calli.

"No. No witch worth their salt wants to come out here to the Frontier, and all the ones already here have a job. The district lords hire up the witches faster than they arrive."

Just what did the district lords want with so many witches? No, never mind. I probably didn't want to know.

"I put the stack of applicants inside your desk drawer in the living room. You can go through them after dinner."

"Goody."

As Calli cooked, I summarized what had gone down tonight: the mark who'd turned out to be a vampire, Jinx, the sheriff, and my suspicions about the district lords being behind the wrong information.

"I wouldn't put it past them," Calli said when I'd finished. "But I'd worry more about that bounty hunter Jinx. He's obviously trailing you, trying to scavenge your work. He's succeeded a few times too."

"Don't remind me," I said. "But at least we have the money for Bella's school now. I'm going to call that a victory and worry about vampires, crime lords, and the scavenging competition later." I took a deep breath. "The food smells delicious."

Calli winked at me. "Of course it does. I made meatballs."

Wow, that was a splurge, but absolutely fitting for our last night all together. I peeked around Calli to check out the other offerings. Sweet potatoes, carrots, green beans… and was that chocolate pudding?

"I love you," I told her earnestly.

"Of course you do." She grinned at me. "Good food is the path to every woman's heart. And man's. You remember that, kid."

I was twenty-two years old and far too old to be a 'kid', but I didn't argue with her. She'd once told us that we'd always be her kids—and I'd come to accept that, even treasure it. It was far better to be someone's kid than to be no one's kid, no matter how old you were.

I snorted. "Sure thing, grams."

Calli was barely forty, but I couldn't help but tease her. I'd learned long ago that the best way to show people you love them was to tease them.

"Come on, Bloody Mary, let's get this food to the table," she said, chuckling.

The rest of the family was already waiting when we brought the food into the dining room, their faces lit up in anticipation. And they didn't waste any time digging in.

"Gods, I'm *starving*," Tessa said, piling a mountain of mashed sweet potatoes onto her plate. "Today was so exhausting."

"What did you do?" I asked her, though I was pretty sure of the answer.

"Gina and I went to the Bazaar."

The Bazaar was the largest shopping mall in town, an even mix of legal and illegal goods. There were clothes and shoes and silly things for teens. If you knew your way around, though, you could find your way to the black market section. I'd ended up there a few times while on the hunt. It was a great place to hide. Everything there looked so weird and suspicious that it was easy for criminals to blend in.

"There were so many people to catch up with, what with school starting up again soon and all. And Mindy Simpson got a tattoo! Can you believe that?"

I didn't have a clue who Mindy Simpson was. Presumably, one of Tessa's two hundred million friends. My sister was the queen bee of Milton High, the most popular girl in school.

"I was thinking of getting one too," Tessa continued. "Just a little one. A rose. Everyone loves a rose." She stole a tentative look at Calli.

"You're not getting a tattoo."

"But Mindy Simpson has one," Tessa protested.

"And does Mindy Simpson understand the health risks of getting a tattoo?"

Tessa pouted out her lips in protest.

"Calli's right," Zane told her. "Have you even looked into the tattoo joints around here? They're filthy. And they reuse the needles."

"Gross," Gin commented. Like Tessa, she was seventeen, but she was the more sensible, more reflective of the two.

Tessa, on the other hand, was all impulse. And stubborn to boot. "Bella could do it. She has all these witchy supplies, and she's a great artist." Tessa shot Bella her winning smile, a smile that could divide nations and crumble an empire. "I just need a little rose and a few letters of text. No biggie for a powerful witch like you."

"Text?" Bella asked.

"A name."

Ah, now the truth was coming out.

"What name?" Calli asked, betraying no hint of emotion.

"Rian. It's really short, see?"

"Who the blazes is Rian?" I asked her.

"My boyfriend," she said proudly.

"Never heard of him."

"You don't know who Rian is? How can you not know who Rian is?" she said, piling on the melodramatics along with the potatoes.

"Uh, maybe because you've never mentioned him?" I replied.

"Oh, I've mentioned him dozens of times. You just never listened."

Right. I turned to Bella. "Have you ever heard of Rian?"

Bella glanced at Tessa, wincing. "The name doesn't ring a bell. But I have been preoccupied lately," she added quickly. She was too nice for her own good.

"I've heard of him," said Gin.

Tessa smiled at her trusty sidekick.

"How long have you been dating?" I asked her.

"A week."

"A week? You've only known him for a week, and you want to permanently tattoo his name on your body? That's so reckless."

"Leda," my little sister replied sternly. "I love you, so don't take this the wrong way, but you really should let go and live a little. Sometimes you need to grab your life by the horns and say, 'You're mine. I am in control of you.' And if that means you have to be impulsive or reckless or whatever it takes to make you feel something, then so be it."

"You know, I think she might be right," Bella told me.

"Of course I am." Tessa grinned at us. "I am very sage."

"So tell us, oh sage one, who is this Rian?" I asked her.

Tessa held up one finger. "First off, he's my soulmate." She popped up a second finger. "And second of all, he's a paranormal soldier. His unit works at the wall. They're all so handsome, so brave and daring, always coming to the aid of people in distress."

"They weren't very brave or daring tonight as they sat

back and watched that vampire beat us bloody," I said. "I can't say anything about how handsome they were, though. They were too busy hiding all the way up on their wall. Maybe I should have shot one of them down to get a look at his handsome face."

"You wouldn't dare!" Tessa exclaimed.

No, I wouldn't, but no one could blame a girl for fantasizing a bit. Being attacked by that vampire had *hurt*. Then again, if the soldiers had helped, we might not have gotten the two thousand dollars. I supposed everything happened for a reason.

"So, when do we get to meet Rian?" I asked, smiling at her.

"That depends. Are you going to try to shoot him?"

"Only if he shoots first."

Before Tessa could do more than look completely horrified, Zane patted his napkin to his lips and said, smooth as silk, "Calli, if I may be excused, I have a date tonight."

"Of course. Who's the lucky girl?"

"Carmen Wilder."

The sheriff's daughter. Wow, he worked fast.

Zane bowed like a prince, then swept out of the room.

"And I think I'd better get started on that big pile of applicants for the witch job," I said, wondering if I'd find even one real witch among them. I turned to Bella. "Care to help me out?"

She nodded. "Of course."

"Good," Calli said, looking at Gin and Tessa. "And you two can do the dishes."

"Dishes?" Tessa groaned. "But we were going to go out and meet up with Rian and his friends."

"You can do that after you clean up," Calli told her.

"You let Zane go out," Tessa pouted.

"Zane and Leda caught a fugitive and earned us two thousand dollars today," she replied calmly. "Today, you two painted your toenails pink and spent a hundred dollars at the Bazaar." She nudged them into the kitchen. "We all have to take our turns working."

"Calli has a funny reward system," I told Bella as we walked into the living room. "My reward for catching that vampire is I get to go through this." I pulled the stack of papers out of my desk drawer and set it down on the coffee table.

"You could go out too," she teased.

"I go out all the time."

"To work. To hunt. You need to live a little."

I held up the first applicant's bundle. "No time."

"You are always working, Leda. You never go see people."

"I went to a bar tonight. There were lots of people there."

"You went there to work. Not for a good time."

Maybe she was right, but I just didn't have time for fun. Zane and I worked in the field, Bella made the potions, and Tessa and Gin helped out when they weren't in school. Calli managed the jobs and the books and still went out on more hunts than the rest of us combined. She was incredible.

But she'd had to be incredible for so long. She'd taken us all in, fed us, loved us, and worked her butt off to make sure we'd have as normal a childhood as anyone post-Scourge could have. She hadn't had a break in over a decade, and one was well overdue. It was our turn to pick up the slack—my turn, since I was the oldest. I had to take more jobs, take some of the load off her shoulders. It was the least I could do after all that she'd given me.

And that wouldn't happen if I wasted my nights away partying. Bella and I had had this conversation before. I wasn't backing down, and she'd never stop trying. That's just what sisters did.

"Taking down that vampire was a good time," I told her. "We made two thousand dollars."

"You'll never meet anyone this way."

"I already know everyone in town. And been hit on by them while they were drunk on moonshine. The highlight of tonight was Dale."

"Dale?" she asked. "As in the grocer next door?"

"The very same."

"Poor guy. Ever since his wife died, he's been so sad."

"He looked really happy locking lips with Cindy tonight." I wiggled my eyebrows at her.

She smiled. "Good for him. I like him. He always lets me take all I want of the Witch's Root and Fairy's Breath from his garden."

Both plants were just weeds to Dale, but they were useful magic potion supplies to a witch like Bella.

"I'm glad you're getting out of here," I told Bella, flipping through the first application. I only had to read a few lines before my worst expectations were realized. Calli was right. No real witch wanted to come here. "And I'm glad that you're getting the chance to study witchcraft." I tossed the first bundle aside, sighing.

"It's just for two years," she said, squeezing my hand. "Then I'll be back."

I threw the next application on the reject pile. The guy thought that being a mega-fan of the *Wild, Wild Witches* comic book series qualified him for the job.

"No, you're going to become a famous witch," I told

Bella. "You'll rise to the head of a coven in five years, no problem."

Bella's laughter rang out, a song of summer and rainbows, a promise that wishes really did come true. "You sure are confident."

"You're good. And I'm glad you're going somewhere where you can get even better."

"Wishing you could come too?"

"No," I said. "I have no special talents. I'm a magical dud."

"No, you're not. You're strong and fast."

"Tell that to the vampire." I winced.

"Leda, you're strong inside, where it counts the most. You don't back down. Ever."

"In other words, I'm stubborn."

"One hundred percent."

I shrugged. "Well, as far as mortal failings go, I could think of a few worse ones."

Bella's laughter was cut short when the door banged open, and Carmen Wilder ran inside, her hair disheveled, her body drenched in sweat, her eyes wide with terror. A stream of unintelligible words poured out of her mouth, punctuated by wheezing heaves of breath.

"Carmen?" Calli asked, rushing to her. "You need to calm down so we can understand you."

"They…took Zane."

I rose to my feet. "Who?"

Carmen's eyes darted erratically around the room, her mind clearly looping inside of a nightmare. "Dark angels. The messengers of hell."

CHAPTER THREE
Gods and Demons

"HERE, DRINK THIS," Bella said to Carmen with a kind smile, handing her a warm cup of milk.

Carmen's hands shook as she took the cup from my sister and lifted it to her mouth, but her jitters slowly quieted, thanks to whatever calming potion Bella had mixed into the milk.

"Can you tell us exactly what happened?" Calli asked, setting her hand on Carmen's shoulder.

"Zane and I had just finished sharing an ice cream sundae at Sweets and Treats. He was walking me home, and we decided to go through the Summer Gardens. He took my hand." A slight smile curled Carmen's lips.

It all sounded so peaceful, so innocent. I paced across the room, knowing it couldn't last.

"Then the dark angels came." The smile wilted from Carmen's mouth. "Four of them. They swooped in on wings as dark as midnight. They grabbed Zane, and then, before I could blink, they were in the air again, flying off with him." Her hands shook, her fear overriding Bella's calming potion. "You have to get him back." She held onto Calli's arm like she was drowning. "You just have to get him back."

"We will," Calli promised, hugging the girl to her.

"Why did they take him?" Sobs burst from Carmen's lips. "Why?"

"The reasons of the dark angels are a mystery."

It was an evasive answer. Calli knew as well as I did why the dark angels would want Zane: for his magic. The angels would have wanted him for the same reason, but as it was, the dark angels had found out first.

A knock sounded on the door, and Bella went to answer. A few moments later, Sheriff Wilder walked into our living room, his heavy boots thumping against the floorboards with every step. As soon as he saw his sobbing daughter, he hurried forward and swooped her up into a comforting hug.

"Thank you for calling me," he told Calli. "And for looking out for my girl. I promise I'll do everything in my power to find Zane."

Calli inclined her head. Then the sheriff and his daughter left.

As soon as they were gone, I turned to Calli. "He won't be able to find Zane, not if the dark angels have him."

Angels were at the top of the Legion of Angels hierarchy, and the dark angels were their counterpart in hell. They served the demons just as the angels served the gods. The Book of the Gods claimed that the demons, desperate to win their war against the gods, set loose the monsters on Earth. And humanity was caught in the middle. Now, two centuries later, Zane was caught in the middle of that same game between gods and demons.

"No, Sheriff Wilder won't be able to find him," Calli agreed. "Zane is out of his reach."

"And is Zane out of *our* reach?" I asked her.

Calli's hard face was answer enough.

"There has to be something we can do," I said desperately.

"What is our rule number one, Leda?" Calli asked.

"That we stick together and always look out for one another."

Bella took my hand.

"And we never give up on one another," Calli said. "We will find a way to get him back."

"They took him because of his magic, didn't they?" Bella said quietly.

Zane was a 'ghost', someone with telepathic magic. It was a really rare ability, one that usually only angels possessed. For a human to be born with that power was almost unheard of. It was one in a hundred million. Or even rarer.

Calli nodded. "Yes."

"But why take him now, all of a sudden?" Bella asked. "Zane has always managed to keep his power hidden before."

"By not using it in public. This is all my fault," I said, my shoulders slouching under the weight of my own guilt.

"Leda—"

"No, Mom. It is. He used his power to disable that vampire tonight. To save me. If I'd been faster or stronger…he'd still be here with us. Someone must have seen him use his magic. The agents of hell have eyes everywhere."

"Don't blame yourself, Leda," said Calli. "We all make our own choices, and Zane chose to use his power to save your life. And he would do it again, even knowing that he'd get captured. You know he would."

I laughed helplessly. "Yeah. He's a fool. Just like all of

us." I plopped onto the sofa.

Bella put her arm around me, rubbing my back.

"What do we do?" Gin said quietly. "How do we get Zane back?"

Calli pulled out her phone, another Magitech splurge that we'd purchased for the family business, and began typing. "We need to get to New York tonight. We need to talk to Rose."

"Rose?" I asked.

"An old friend. She is a telepath."

"Will she be able to track Zane?" asked Tessa.

"I hope so, dear. I really do. Because it's the only chance we have of saving him."

◆ ◇ ◆ ◇ ◆

We were supposed to leave for New York tomorrow morning to see Bella off to school, but Calli managed to get our train tickets changed to tonight. So after quickly packing Bella's bags, we all headed to the train station.

From the outside, the train waiting to bring us to New York was sleek, skinny, and shiny—a masterpiece of modern magical engineering. Powered by Magitech, it could make the journey of five hundred miles in just under an hour.

The inside of the train was more nostalgic than modern, a throwback to an earlier era. Rows of large benches, covered with a luxurious layer of red velvet, were bolted to a hardwood floor. On either side of the train carriage, large glass windows framed in wood provided a view of the passing landscapes, though it was too dark outside to see much at the moment. Elegant iron lanterns dangled from the ceiling, swaying gently as the train sped along to its destination.

Calli shared a bench with Tessa and Gin, and Bella and I sat together the next row back. Bella had changed out of her summer dress in favor of a very smart skirt suit in the witch style. The hip-hugging pencil skirt was navy blue. So was the fitted jacket she wore over a cream-colored blouse. A brooch with the witch's rune for knowledge was pinned at the blouse's neckline. Black knee-high laced boots and white gloves topped off her wardrobe, and her strawberry-blonde hair was pulled up into a lovely twist.

"You look perfect," I told her. "You're going to blow them all away."

Bella smoothed out a crease in her skirt, then refolded her hands on her lap. "I hope you're right."

"You were made for this, Bella. One hundred percent."

Bella laughed. It was a very well-mannered laugh. The witches of the New York University of Witchcraft, themselves very proper ladies and gentlemen, would have approved. Witchcraft wasn't just about mixing potions to cast complex spells. It was about doing it in style. Of all the branches of supernatural society, the witches were the most dignified, the most chic. Bella embodied this ideal, right down to the corset she was wearing. It had taken a good half hour for me and Bella to figure out that piece of bone-crunching engineering and get her into it. The process had involved a great deal of pushing, pulling, contorting, and swearing. From me. Bella had borne it all with dignity and grace, even though I was sure it must have hurt her at least as much as it had hurt me.

"Can you breathe in that thing?" I asked her.

"As long as I sit up really straight."

I laughed.

"I'm sure one gets used to it after a while," she added.

"Or one loses all feeling in the midsection."

"I'm sure there's a potion to help with that."

Just then, the man with the snack cart rolled past, and we each ordered a cinnamon roll and a cup of coffee. We would need an abundance of sugar and caffeine if we were going to make it through this long night.

We arrived at the New York City train station promptly at two o'clock in the morning. Though it was the middle of the night, the station was bustling with activity, passengers rushing this way and that, getting on and off of trains. I'd been to the city a few times before, and every time was just the same. Just as fast and frenzied. Just as overwhelming. Calli led the way through the station, fearless as ever.

"Amazing," Tessa said, looking up at the station's high ceilings, beautifully arched and crafted from glass.

Gin nodded. This was their first time here, and pure wonder shone through their eyes. And if I took a moment to overlook the crowds overwhelming my senses, I couldn't help but appreciate the station's beauty too. It was as stylish as the train, that same mix of nostalgic elegance and modern style. Beautiful white marble floors spread out in every direction.

A painted scene out of Earth's history covered each and every wall, the timeline progressing as we made our way through the station. It began with the monsters overrunning the Earth. Next came a scene of the gods coming down to save humanity, giving us gifts of magic and technology. The new army of supernaturals followed. Several walls featured their battles against the monsters, driving them away, deep into the world's Wastelands. Paintings showed new cities growing and old ones being rebuilt. A new society was born, one with supernaturals in it.

The final hall of paintings was grander and more colorful than the rest. On the ceilings, the gods sat on their thrones in the clouds. The walls showed the angels in their terrible, gorgeous glory. No human could be that beautiful—or that cruel.

Light shone down from the gods' on the ceiling, illuminating the angels in shimmering streams of glitter and magic. Their wings twinkled like diamond snowflakes. They shone like rainbows and sparkled like the ocean. And they glowed like fire. Each angel held a sword and a shield, which they used to battle the monsters and demons surrounding groups of frightened humans. A repeating line of text below the angels read, 'The shield of the gods' mercy, the sword of the gods' justice.' It was very beautifully-painted propaganda.

We walked under the arched exit of the train station, passing witches in their tights and skirts, boots and feathered hats. The male witches wore vests or long coats, and an assortment of other accessories like canes, top hats, goggles, and pocket watches. The witches were the world's engineers and inventors, scientists and doctors, pilots and professors—and all that thinking and tinkering they did in style.

They weren't the only ones walking the streets tonight. Vampires were out in full force. Like Mark, they wore silk and leather. Their hair was perfectly styled; their skin seemed to shimmer in the moonlight. They walked in groups, flashing charming smiles at anyone who caught their interest.

"Good evening, my dear," one of them said to me. His eyes had taken on that distinctive silver-blue sheen. His friends' eyes had turned too, and they were all staring at my hair.

A vampire had once told me that my hair shimmered like white gold in the moonlight. He'd also mentioned that there was something about it that mesmerized vampires. And he was right. Most vampires who saw it were hit with an irresistible urge to touch it, which would inevitably lead to them trying to use my neck as a chew toy. I guess I was lucky that Mark hadn't been as affected as these fellows here.

"You'd best be moving along," Calli said, stepping between me and the vampires.

The vampires blinked down hard a few times, shaking free of whatever trance they'd been in.

"No offense intended, ma'am," one of the vampires said to Calli.

They all bowed, then continued on their way, careful to divert their eyes from me. Smart. The Legion of Angels didn't intervene in minor affairs of the human world, but as soon as supernaturals stopped playing by the rules, they came down with an iron fist. Vampires feeding on people without their permission was one of those rules. Luckily for the vampires, there were more than enough people who wanted to be fed on. Those vampire groupies didn't realize that behind every one of those perfect faces lay a monster, just waiting to come unhinged—and a hunger deep within that could never be satiated. That was the ugly side of the beautiful vampires. And it was shocking how quickly things could get ugly.

My pulse still pounding from that close call with the vampires, I put on a tough face and followed behind Calli. Bella reached over and squeezed my hand.

"Maybe I should start wearing a hat," I whispered.

"I wonder what it is about your hair that attracts them," she whispered back.

I winked at her. "Vampires like blondes."

"No, it isn't that. It's something…magical, I think."

Maybe she was right. Maybe this was my magic ability: to be catnip for vampires. As far as magical abilities went, it really kind of sucked. Why couldn't I shoot fire out of my hands instead? That was at least useful. It was at least a real gift. Being irresistible to blood-sucking vampires was nothing but a curse.

We waited while Calli had Bella's bags sent ahead to the university. She put Gin and Tessa in a cab next and sent them to an old friend back from her days of working for the League, the world's largest bounty-hunting company. The girls pleaded and whined, but Calli didn't bend. For good reason too. Where we were headed was no place for them.

So Calli, Bella, and I headed away from the train station. After a few blocks, the brightly-lit modern facades gave way to darker, dirtier buildings and streets. There, in the middle of the city's red light district, we found Rose's shop.

A flashy sign—one of a crystal ball with pink smoke coming out of it—advertised psychic readings. It blinked and buzzed in a rapid, almost dizzying rhythm, winding up my senses so tightly that I had to look away. I concentrated on the door instead. An odd symbol—that of an opening flower with looping, never-ending layers—was painted on the wood. But that's not what I was looking at.

I was looking at the door itself. It was partially open. Calli frowned, pushing it further open. We followed her inside.

Furniture was overturned all around the room, like there had been a fight. Blood was everywhere—on the carpets, the walls, dripping down the purple satin tablecloth of the round table with the crystal ball. And amongst all the chaos, a woman lay in a pool of her own blood.

CHAPTER FOUR
Ghosts

ROSE WAS ALIVE. But just barely. As Bella tried to revive her with a tincture, I turned to Calli.

"Whoever did this knew you knew her. And knew we'd be coming," I said. "Zane's kidnapping and this are linked."

"You know what I always say about coincidences."

I nodded. "That they don't exist. Not in our world. Not after all that we've seen. There is always someone pulling the strings. This isn't a coincidence; it's a full-on conspiracy."

"Someone wants Zane," Calli declared. "And that someone doesn't want us to find him."

"But how did this someone know you know Rose?"

Calli frowned, cursing something about dark angels under her breath. The messengers of hell had eyes everywhere. Ears everywhere.

"She's regaining consciousness," Bella told us. "But she doesn't have long. Her injuries are beyond medicine or magic, at least any we have at our disposal."

Calli looked down. Bella had wrapped a blanket around Rose, and she was holding her hand.

"Can we move her to the witches hospital?" Calli asked.

"She wouldn't survive the trip," Bella said.

I squatted down beside Rose. The telepath was blinking back into consciousness with obvious reluctance. She looked like she'd rather we hadn't woken her before death. One glance at her injuries was all it took to understand why. Rose hadn't just been attacked; she'd been completely brutalized. Her ribs were broken, her legs dangling at unnatural angles. Deep lacerations covered her chest and midsection, and there was a noticeable gash in her head. Whoever had done this, they hadn't wanted her to survive.

"It's a wonder she's still alive now." Bella's voice cracked.

"The killer must have just left," Calli said.

Rose coughed out a wet laugh. "The bastard didn't take into account my resilience. I'm tough."

"Who was it?" Calli asked her, taking her other hand.

"A dark angel. I didn't see much of him. He was in the shadows. But I felt his magic. Hell-bending, end-of-the-world magic."

"What did he want?"

Rose paled. "For me to die. He knew you were coming to see me."

"He said that?" Calli asked.

"Yes. He said he couldn't let me help you find Zane."

"They knew you were our best hope for getting Zane back, for tracking him down," Calli said.

"Our *only* hope," I added.

"No." Rose coughed up blood. "Not the only way."

She and Calli exchanged loaded looks. They remained still for a few moments, neither saying a word.

"No," Calli said finally. "That is *not* an option."

"Your boy is in danger, Calli."

"Can you find him?" I asked her.

Rose shook her head. "I caught only glimpses of him

being taken away. Flashes."

"We brought something of his with us." I reached into the pocket of my jeans and dug out an amulet. I held it out to her. "It will help you connect to him, right? That's how this kind of magic works, isn't it?"

Rose looked at the amulet in my hand and shook her head. "No, it's not that simple. I'm not that powerful of a telepath. In order to link to someone, I need to have a connection to them. The stronger that connection is, the more I see. I don't know him well enough. I've never met him. My connection to him is only through Calli. I can't give you more than I have, more than those flashes of dark angels taking him."

"Can't you try glimpsing him again?" I asked, taking her hands in desperation. "Can't you give us hints of where he is now? Maybe it will be enough for us to find him."

Rose coughed up more blood. "I'm sorry. Maybe if I weren't so weak right now…but I just can't."

Calli set her hands on my shoulders. "We will find a way," she promised.

I looked at Rose. She knew something. I knew she did. But I couldn't press her for information now, not as long as Calli was standing nearby. I didn't know what Rose knew that could help us, but whatever it was, Calli wouldn't allow it. Maybe it was some kind of dark magic. I had to get Rose alone, to figure out what she knew. If it meant saving my brother, I'd do whatever I had to.

The call of approaching police sirens bellowed outside.

"Stay here," Calli said, heading for the door.

Rose moaned in pain.

"What can I do to help?" Bella asked her.

"I have some drops. The vial is in the back."

"Of course. I'll be right back."

The ropes of beads hanging in the doorway leading to the back jingled as Bella pushed through them. Rose watched her leave, then turned her eyes on me.

"What do you know?" I asked her. "How do I save Zane?"

"Calli doesn't want me to say."

"But you want to tell me."

"That boy means a lot to Calli, to all of you," she said.

"Yes. And I will do whatever it takes to save him," I declared.

Rose nodded slowly. "I saw that in your eyes. Your brother is a ghost, a telepath. That's why they want him. There are rules in place about us ghosts. We're not free to live our lives as others are. When discovered, we must be turned over to the gods. They think ghosts are the key to defeating the demons. If they can just get enough of us."

"The demons think so too."

"The gods, the demons. He is worth a lot to a lot of people," said Rose. "Ghosts can only stay hidden for so long. I stayed under the radar by peddling my powers with all the dramatic flair of a quack. Sometimes the best hiding spot is in plain sight."

"But someone found out about you," I said, glancing at her wounds.

"Yes. As I said, tricks might buy us a few years, but they always find out. It's not a question of *if*. It's a question of *when*. And of *who*, gods or demons."

"Why did they try to kill you?" I asked. "If you're so valuable, why didn't the dark angels bring you with them?"

"I am not a powerful telepath, I fear." She frowned, as though embarrassed. "They only came here to prevent me from helping you. I wasn't worth the effort of bringing along. The gods and demons are collecting the most powerful telepaths in the world. I would just dilute the bloodline. And I'm too old to breed for them."

"They are breeding telepaths?"

It was appalling, but somehow I wasn't surprised. Not one bit. People worshipped the gods, but even as a child, I'd begun to wonder if the only difference between them and the demons was who had won the war. Of course, I'd never said it aloud. The demons weren't the only ones who had eyes and ears everywhere.

"Yes, they're breeding us," said Rose.

"But why?"

She shook her head. "I have no idea. But whatever it is, it can't be good."

"If I can get Zane back, we'll run, somewhere far away. Somewhere neither gods nor demons can find us."

A ghost of a smile touched her lips. "You are a good sister to him."

"I would do anything to save him."

"I hope so," she replied. "Because there's only one way for you to find him. And you're not going to like it."

"Tell me. Please." I squeezed her hands.

"You have to join the Legion of Angels."

CHAPTER FIVE
The Legion of Angels

AS SOON AS I heard it, I realized Rose was right. The gods bestowed powers on the soldiers of the Legion. One of those powers was Ghost's Whisper, the ability to connect telepathically to those close to you, no matter how far away they were. No other ghost in the world could help us find Zane because no other ghost knew him. So I would just have to gain the ability I needed myself. The solution was so simple, and yet so impossible. So dangerous, so deadly, so insane. It might just work.

But Calli would *never* go for it. Not in a million years. Which was why I wasn't going to tell her.

Bella came back with a glass vial. She was crouching down to give Rose a few drops from the bottle when the ghost began spasming. I held to her hands, trying to steady her, but her convulsions were too wild. I couldn't hold her still. The drops splattered across her face, never making it into her mouth.

Calli hurried into the room with two paranormal police officers and a trio of witches. They were too late. Calli stood by in stone-faced silence as her friend breathed out her final breaths—and then she was just gone.

Beside me, Bella was weeping sadly. I wrapped my arm around my sister, hugging her to me. She'd always been sensitive. So sweet, so kind. It made her perfect for the job of healer, but it wouldn't help her in the Legion. Of all of us, only I could join. I was the only one with any chance of making it in the Legion. Calli had always said I was stubborn and hardheaded. That stubbornness might be my only chance of surviving the Legion. Many of their initiates never lived past the first stage. No, best not think about that. I needed to use that strong, stubborn will of mine, to wrap it around myself like a cloak, like a shield. And never let anything pierce it.

We stood there for another few hours as the police questioned us. Calli did the talking. She didn't mention anything about Zane or dark angels, only that we'd come to see an old friend before bringing Bella to school. They didn't question us further. They expressed their sympathies, then the witches carried away Rose's body.

The sun was rising on New York by the time we finally stepped outside again. We headed over to see Calli's friend Sam, who was looking after Tessa and Gin. Sam lived above a diner she owned, and when we arrived, the former bounty hunter was frying up pancakes. We joined her and the girls for a solemn sunrise breakfast, then walked over to the New York University of Witchcraft.

The city's premier school for witchcraft was awash with style. The campus was made up of five buildings situated around a flower garden in the middle that grew all the ingredients the students might need. Each building looked like a very large mansion—or a small castle. We took a path lined with rose trees and a pond of sculptures on our way to Building 3. The sculptures dug and dipped, scooping up water and spraying it out in a dance of mechanical movements.

Inside Building 3, which housed the dormitories, a glossy wood floor shone in the morning light pouring in from the windows. Twin grandiose staircases embellished with red runners arched up to the next level. A standing vase exploding with colorful summer flowers stood on either side of the staircases, and gold bannisters curved gracefully along the edges. Chandeliers alight with enchanted flames dripped down from the high ceilings. I felt like I was inside of a fairytale.

Except this wasn't my fairytale. It was Bella's. My path led in a very different direction.

We brought Bella upstairs, quickly finding her room. It was modest compared to the grand entrance hall downstairs, but I liked it even more. The pieces of furniture were all antiques. Each and every one of them had a history, if only you could find it. There were two desks and a bed on either side of the room. A small bathroom lay between, decked out with a myriad of complex shower appliances.

"I wonder when my roommate will arrive," said Bella, looking around with excitement. "And if she'll like me."

"Everyone likes you," I told my sister. "But just try not to snore."

"I don't…" A smile curled her lips. "You're teasing me again."

"I have to get it all out of my system now. I won't be seeing you for a while." *If ever.*

Bella watched Calli and our younger sisters step onto the balcony, then she turned to me. "Leda, what's wrong?"

Oh, nothing. I'm just about to give up my life. But all I said was, "I'm sad to see you leave."

Bella smiled at me. "I will never leave. I'll always be

your sister. Our bond is stronger than blood, stronger than magic. You remember that."

Then she gave me a look that made me swear she must have had some inkling that I was about to do something crazy. She was right.

"Hey, Bella, you have got to have a look at your balcony," Tessa said, coming back inside. "It's so grand. So romantic. You'll be like a princess in a castle, looking down on your kingdom."

"A kingdom of Fairy's Breath and Dragon's Bark," said Calli, smiling. "It's a lovely view."

"The windows are resistant to attacks both magical and mundane," Gin added with a shy smile. "And there's a spyglass that allows you to look all across the grounds and even into the city."

Gin often helped Calli out in the garage, taking care of our vehicles and weapons. She had quite a knack for the work.

I gave Bella one last hug, then stepped back, my eyes stinging with unshed tears. "You're going to do great."

Gin, then Tessa, then finally Calli hugged her too. After that, we left her to settle in before the school's orientation session began.

"I have a few supplies to pick up before our train leaves," Calli said as we returned to the street.

We'd decided to go home and think up a plan to save Zane. Well, actually, Calli had decided, and I just hadn't said anything. I already had a plan, but if I shared it, Calli would try to stop me. My plan was the only way, even though it meant going back on my promise to take over more of the family business. Zane was family too. I couldn't just let the demons have him.

"You go along," I told Calli and my sisters. "I want to

check out the Armory." I tapped the glass window of the shop in front of me, one of many in a chain that had locations all over the world. "The New York Armory is supposed to be the largest one in all of North America. They've got to have a great selection. After my run-in with the vampire last night, I want to take a look at their latest in anti-vampire weaponry."

I thought my lie was convincing enough, but Calli gave me a funny look.

"What's my budget?" I asked her hastily, hoping that would make my story more plausible.

Calli continued to watch me for a moment before she said, "Try to stay below five hundred dollars."

"Will do," I replied, then turned to pretend to look at the weapons featured in the display window.

I waited until Calli and the girls turned the corner, then I hurried off toward the Promenade. Gods, I felt like a teenager again playing out a deception.

The Promenade was a street full of towering office buildings that housed branches of many of the world's major organizations. The League, the worldwide bounty hunting company, occupied a slate—nearly black—building next to the blue glass skyscraper that was home to the paranormal soldiers. And past that, smack dab in the middle of the Promenade, was a sparkling white obelisk, the east coast headquarters of the Legion of Angels.

I took a deep breath and walked toward the front door with a confident gait, as though I were not completely scared out of my mind.

The obelisk's interior did not live up to the outside's foreboding architecture. It wasn't as sparse as the paranormal soldiers' buildings either. The lobby was opulent, drowning in heavenly tones of gold and white with occasional accents from all across the color spectrum. Like in the long hall of the train station, paintings of grand and powerful gods covered the ceiling. Painted angels stood at the edge between ceiling and wall, guarding the border. Vampires, shifters, fairies, and many other supernaturals came next, filling the walls.

Two Legion soldiers in brown khakis, tank tops, and heavy boots cut across my path, pulling a struggling, shackled, shrieking vampire toward the back. The people working behind the large, curved reception desk didn't even look up. This must have been a regular occurrence around here. The twin doors leading to a back area swooshed open. The soldiers and their vampire passed through, and then the doors closed, swallowing the vampire's screams.

Two Legion soldiers, both dressed in black leather, walked side-by-side toward the doors—each one with a sword on his back, each one donning a small metallic insignia of a fire symbol on his chest.

I returned my attention to the reception desk. There, another Legion soldier was getting a chocolate chip cookie from the plate on the counter while she made smalltalk with the secretary about dragon sightings. I walked up to the desk, my steps faltering as I crossed the icy marble expanse. I waited at the desk until the secretary was done chatting with the cookie-loving Legion soldier.

"Yes?" the secretary asked, locking her stern eyes on me.

"I'd like to join the Legion." I tried to sound strong as I said it, but my voice just came out so weak and pathetic.

The secretary and the cookie soldier looked me over, as though assessing me, then they exchanged amused looks. It appeared they weren't impressed with what they saw.

"Sit over there and fill this out." The secretary passed me a clipboard over the desk. "Bring it back when you're done." Then she turned away from me and started up a conversation with the cookie soldier about recent vampire attacks.

Thus dismissed, I headed over to the seating area. There were five other people sitting here, each of them busily filling out their own forms. Except my forms were yellow and theirs green. I seemed to remember green was the color for those petitioning the Legion for aid. Yellow was…I don't know, a warning. But I guess it was better than red. Or putting a skull and crossbones on the cover sheet.

The people with the green sheets looked even more nervous than I felt, if that were even possible. The thing was anyone could petition the Legion of Angels for aid, but very few received it. The Legion was more selective about which petitions they took than which initiates they welcomed into their doors. They knew the weak initiates wouldn't survive the first month anyway.

Stop thinking like that! I chided myself as I began filling out my application.

Ten pages and one hundred questions later, I handed the clipboard back to the secretary, then went back to sit and wait on my really uncomfortable but very pretty chair. I shook out my hand. It was sore from all the writing. These weren't multiple choice questions. Each one was like an essay, an exposé into a corner of my life. They wanted to know everything: health, history, education, magic. I didn't know why they bothered. The Legion had never rejected any application to join their army. But they were a government agency, and the one thing government agencies were united in was their love of bureaucracy. It must have made them feel good to file away another big stack of papers.

The minutes bled by. One by one, the petitioners were

called into the back. Most of them returned looking distraught. Their petitions had obviously been rejected. One person came back looking happy, the lucky guy of the day.

Finally, when there was no one else left in the seating area, a man in a business suit waved me forward. I followed him into the back, and we walked in silence past closed doors until we reached an open room at the end. He waited for me to take a seat in front of the unoccupied desk, then without a word, he turned and left, closing the door behind him.

Trying not to feel like I'd been called into the principal's office for bad behavior, I tapped my heels against the chair and waited. Again. My stomach growled in protest. Those pancakes felt like eons ago.

After a few minutes, I swiped a pen from a glass jar full of them. I didn't see any paper to doodle on, so I began tapping against my chair instead. Something told me the Legion frowned upon desk graffiti.

Two-hundred-and-sixteen taps later, the door opened.

"Finally," I said, sighing. "I thought you'd forgotten about me."

"We do not forget anything," a man's voice said, crisp and proper, each word pulsing with raw power.

I turned and looked up into the face of an angel. Literally.

I didn't know how I knew what he was. After all, he didn't have his wings out. But I just knew. Magic slid off of him like a cloak, igniting the air between us. My skin buzzed, goosebumps prickling up. Whatever vibes he was putting out, my body was two hundred percent tuned in. I just couldn't decide if I was intrigued or scared shitless of him.

He certainly was handsome. No, not just handsome—astonishingly beautiful. And frightening. Just like all of the angels. His hair shone like caramel. It fell partially over his eyes, just long enough to be charming without turning disorderly. He wore the standard Legion uniform: a leather bodysuit. As black as ink, it looked like it had been melted onto his body. Every dip, every curve of muscle was visible beneath it. I couldn't help but cast a long appreciative look down the length of him, and for one moment I almost forgot how dangerous angels were.

But then reality set in. Some men worked out so they'd look good. This man worked out so he could kill people. He looked strong enough to snap me in half over the desk if he decided to—and there wasn't a damn thing I could do about it. He had a body no mortal could possess—and a soul so hard that it burned cold and unyielding from behind his emerald eyes. As his gaze met mine, I froze, mesmerized.

"Why do you want to join the Legion?" He sat down opposite me, sliding the pen from my frozen fingers.

I felt like I was in a daze. That's what people said about angels. That they put you into a trance. I snapped myself out of it.

"I wrote it all there," I told him, nodding toward the clipboard in his hands. My application was snapped to it.

His perfect brows drew together like he was surprised. Maybe people didn't ever talk back to him.

"You wrote that you want to keep the world safe from rogue supernaturals," he said.

I folded my hands together and smiled at him. "That's not a good reason?"

"It is *a* reason," he replied. "In fact, it's the reason roughly seventy percent of applicants write on their form."

I kept on smiling, even as my teeth began to hurt. "That's me. Conformist, obedient, toeing the straight and narrow line."

He looked like I'd just spit acid in his gods-ordained eyes. "Is that supposed to be funny?"

I struggled to hold onto the smile. "No."

"You work for a bounty hunting company called Pandora's Box." His eyebrow twitched up at the name, almost like he was amused. Or maybe he was just allergic to me.

"My Mom and sisters and I run it. Estrogen-fueled, you know."

His eyebrow twitch didn't repeat. Apparently, I wasn't all that funny after all.

"Your foster mother, Callista Pierce. And foster sisters, Bellatrix, Tessa, and Ginnifer Pierce."

"You looked me up. Aw, I'm flattered. And I don't even know your name."

"Your foster brother Zane Pierce is also a member of the business," he continued on.

I struggled to remain calm. Talking about Zane would just make trouble. I tried to sidestep the issue with a smile and a joke. "We call Zane the Wild Card, the only man in the group."

The angel's face was carved from granite, a statue of bone-crunching might. Like the statues of angels in the town halls and city centers.

"Why do you want to join the Legion?" he repeated his question.

"I already told you."

"There's more to it," he said. "I can feel it."

"Well, your angel senses must be backfiring because that's all there is. You've seen my record. I help people, even when I'd make more money if I didn't. I can't help myself."

He narrowed his eyes at me. "Your record does seem to confirm that."

"See?" I said, continuing to smile. Man, I really needed to work out those facial muscles. My endurance was crap. "As I said, I'm a loyal—"

"You have never expressed interest in joining the Legion before," he cut in. "How old are you?"

My smile wobbled. "My birthday is listed right there."

"I know. I want to hear you say it."

"Twenty-two."

"And?"

"And what?" I sighed.

He just looked at me, daring me to defy him.

"Twenty-two and five months," I told him. "Should I scribble my cup size on there too while I'm at it?"

Proving that angels weren't human, his eyes didn't even dip to my chest. "No need. You will be measured by our staff for your uniform."

"So that means I'm in?"

"Not yet."

Geez, the Legion didn't reject anyone. Why was this guy giving me a hard time?

"The Legion accepts initiates starting on the first day you turn twenty-two," he said coolly. "Why wait five months if you're so eager to serve?"

"Sorry I'm late. I wanted to see my sister off to school before I left. Which I did early this morning, then came straight here."

He didn't look like he was buying my load of bullshit. Damn, I'd had it all worked out. It had sounded so convincing in my head.

"Why do you want to join the Legion?"

I was beginning to hate that question with the fury of a thousand burning hells. "I hear angels are great in the sack," I told him, proud of myself for keeping a straight face as I said it.

My words made him pause for a few seconds as he stared at me in silence. "I will find out what you're hiding," he said calmly, lacing his fingers together. "You can be sure of that."

"Honey, I usually save interrogations for the second date."

His nostrils flared, and the air crackled with magic. "If you're to survive the Legion, you will need to watch that mouth."

"Does that mean I'm in?"

He continued to stare at me for a few seconds, then he stood from the desk and opened the door. "Follow me," he said over his shoulder.

I followed him back down the hall, wondering what this was all about. Maybe I'd mouthed off too much this time. "Taking me outside to shoot me while the city looks on?" I asked.

"No."

He led me through the double doors into the lobby, then out the front door. We walked for a few blocks, the crowds parting before him. Either they were as scared of him as I should have been, or he was using his magic to influence them.

He stopped in front of a club with a flashing sign out front. Their logo appeared to be a heart with a wing flapping on either side. Whatever this place was, it was popular. It was—I glanced up at the nearest clocktower—ten in the morning, and the line into the club extended around the block. My angelic companion walked right to the front. The bouncer took one look at him, then waved us inside. The bouncer seemed to know him. Of course he did. There weren't a lot of angels in the world. If this angel was stationed here, everyone in the city must have known who he was.

Even though it was full daylight outside, inside the club, night was in full swing. Disco lights spun and flashed in every direction, bouncing off the gyrating bodies of the dancers on the dance floor. A few of the women stopped to smile and wave their panties at my angel. What the hell kind of place had he brought me to?

"I was just kidding about the date, you know," I said as we sat down at the bar.

He gave me a frosty look. "This isn't a date."

Something in his eyes made me blush. I couldn't explain it. It must have been more angel magic at work.

"You brought me to a club," I pointed out. "That seems like a date to me." I just couldn't help myself. My mouth was running away with me again.

"This is your interview," he stated.

"Here?" I looked around at the club full of daylight-shunning partiers.

"Yes, here. A lot of rogue vampires have been popping up in the city over the past few months. Someone is making them outside of the system."

Uh-oh. The gods didn't like that. They crushed all vampire-turning operations outside their control and punished the responsible party. Without mercy.

"I just captured one of those vampires who got away," I told the angel.

"I know. That's why I'm confident this test should be no problem for you."

Just how much had he read up on me? We hadn't

reported Zane's disappearance for obvious reasons, but what if the Legion had other sources? They'd start asking why the dark angels took him. And I didn't have a good answer for them.

I tried to cover my nervousness with a smile. "So confident in my abilities? If I didn't know better, I might think you're flirting with me."

"Then it's a good thing you know better. You're obviously smarter than you look."

I didn't know whether or not to be offended by that comment, so I said nothing more. In the meantime, the angel celebrated my silence by motioning to the exhausted bartender. The poor guy looked like his shift had been over for a long time, but my companion's attention woke him right back up. He quickly put down two glasses of silver liquid in front of us. It didn't look like alcohol—or anything else that I'd ever seen. It rippled strangely, like it wasn't entirely liquid.

"There's a rogue vampire in the bathroom, sipping on the replacement bartender's neck," the angel said, swirling his drink around with total calmness. "You will apprehend him. *Apprehend*, not kill. I want him alive."

"I don't have the right gear on me to take on a vampire," I protested.

"You have everything you need."

He looked across my body. I might have thought he was checking me out, but he'd had plenty of time to do that already and hadn't even tried. Besides, his gaze was more assessing, calculating. Like he was looking at a weapon. I paused uncertainly.

He pushed the second drink at me. "Drink."

"What is it? Some kind of angel drink?"

"It's vodka. With a little magic added in."

I stared into the glass. Good enough for me. I threw back my head and emptied the magic vodka down my throat. It burned even worse than regular vodka.

"This is some nasty shit," I told him, coughing.

"Do hurry," he replied. "The girl doesn't have much time before the vampire kills her."

"Then why don't you help her? That's your job."

"And this is your test," he said coldly.

Cursing the inhumanity of angels, I pushed away from the bar and headed for the door that led to the bathrooms. He just sat there, watching me. Growling under my breath, I opened the door into a dark hallway. As I entered the ladies' room, I heard a wet slurping noise. I could see feet shuffling in feeble protest under one of the stalls. I paused in the doorway, considering my options.

If I attacked him outright, the victim might get hurt. I had to lure the bloodsucker out of the stall. And to do that, I needed to present him with a more appealing target. With that decided, I allowed the door to slam shut, then I walked across the bathroom, my boots echoing off the tiled floor.

The slurping ceased. I stopped in front of the sink and turned on the water. I heard the brush of fabric, like he was wiping his mouth against clothing. He slid out of the stall, and I turned around. He was blocking my view of the inside of the stall. I hoped the woman was ok.

The vampire swaggered toward me, smiling. He had that glow vampires got after feeding, like their skin was shining from the inside.

"Hey, darling," he said, trying to dazzle me with his charming smile. I didn't see any blood on his mouth, so he must have wiped his mouth on his victim's clothes. Yuck.

He was moving like he was a bit drunk. Must have been a new vampire. It took more than sipping on one victim to get an older one drunk. And this one was clearly drunk. Good. It would make him slow and sloppy. Maybe I would even survive this.

"Hello," I said, smiling back. "Looking for a good time?"

I brushed my hair off of my neck. His gaze darted from my throat, to my hair, then back to my throat again—around and around again, like he couldn't decide which one he wanted more. His eyes did eventually hone in on my pulse. Which was really pounding fast right at the moment. I tried to calm myself. Getting nervous would just make my blood pump faster, which would only excite the vampire even more.

He glided forward, closing the distance between us in an instant. Some people would have been impressed, even awed by that, but those people were too blind to see vampires for what they really were: monsters.

The monster before me reached out, brushing his hand down my hair. "So beautiful. Like a silver waterfall." A smirk quirked his lips. "Shame I have to stain it."

He dipped his head to my neck with leisurely slowness, apparently confident that I would be easy prey. I loved to prove people wrong. Before his fangs had descended, I smashed my knee hard into his groin. As he doubled over, I sidestepped and pushed him headfirst into the mirror. Glass shattered, pouring all over the sink. Dazed, the vampire stumbled back. I grabbed one of the mirror shards and stabbed him in the neck. He howled with rage, blood gushing out of the wound. He staggered forward like a beast, and I ducked to avoid the heavy swipes he swung at my head.

"You will pay for that," he snarled, tearing the shard out of his neck.

He rushed forward, trying to grab me, but he was still too dazed and drunk. Though the rage was quickly burning off the blood high. I didn't have much time. I grabbed the fire extinguisher off the wall and sprayed him in the face. Sometimes a strength could be a weakness. The vampire's enhanced senses meant he felt the pain that much more. He howled in agony, blindly scratching at his eyes. I swung the fire extinguisher, hitting him hard over the head. He crumpled to the floor.

I was about to check on the victim when two more vampires entered the bathroom from the other door.

"Hey, Derek, are you done suck—"

The new arrivals froze when they saw the unconscious vampire at my feet. I had a split of a second, and I took it. I barged out of the first door, sprinting down the hallway to enter the main club area. The vampires were hot on my heels, shoving dancers and drunks aside to get at me. The crowd scrambled, people fleeing for the exit, knocking over speakers, chairs, and one another in their mad dash to be the first one out the door.

The vampires went straight for me. I jumped at the bar. The bartender had abandoned his post when the mayhem hit the dance floor, so the bar was empty. I slid over the top and ducked for cover as a vampire's fist swung at me. I smashed a bottle down on his hand, drenching him in liquor. Then I reached for the matches under the counter and set that bloodsucker on fire.

He stumbled back, then ran for the nearest wall, trying to put out the flames by banging himself against it. Repeatedly. I left him to it, and poured another bottle of alcohol over a dish towel, which I set ablaze as I tossed it over the other vampire's head. He tried to pry it off, but the flames had already spread across his body.

The two vampires ran around the now-abandoned club, howling and shrieking and burning. The flames wouldn't kill them—they were too resilient for that—but it did keep them busy. I grabbed a hot saucepan from the cooking area and knocked one, then the other, over the head with it. They fell to the floor.

A slow, steady clap echoed in the empty room, punching through the silence. I turned to see the angel walking toward me and the two sleeping beauties at my feet.

"Thanks for helping," I said with a fake smile, tossing the saucepan aside.

He looked from me, to the unconscious vampires, to the debris of glass and fire all across the club. "What the hell was that?"

I stomped down a flame on one of the vampires. "That's how I fight."

He was shaking his head like he'd never seen anything so inappropriate. So uncouth.

"We don't have time to argue about my fighting style. We need to help the woman in the back."

I hurried to the bathroom, surprised when he followed me. I knelt down in front of the woman, feeling for a pulse. She still had one!

"Move aside," the angel told me.

I did as he asked, and he lowered down beside her. As he set his hands on her stomach, magic glowed from them, washing across her whole body. The woman's wounds healed before my eyes. She blinked down a few times, her eyes slowly focusing.

"An angel," she gasped, adoration washing across her face as she stared up at the glowing angel.

She was positively mesmerized, so much so that if he'd

asked her to stab herself in the chest, she'd have done it without hesitation. Honestly, I didn't see the appeal of the man. Sure, he was handsome—ok, so he was the most gorgeous man I'd ever seen—but he was also an asshole. I didn't tell the woman that this beautiful angel had been prepared to just let her die. She had suffered enough for one night. She deserved a moment of happiness.

The angel stood, leaving me holding the woman. I helped her to her feet.

"Are you all right?" I asked her as the object of her undying devotion left the bathroom.

She glanced down at the sleeping vampire on the floor and shuddered. "Fine."

"You should get out of here," I told her.

She nodded and walked toward the door, giving the vampire a wide berth. I shot the bloodsucker at my feet a look of pure loathing. He'd tried to stain my hair red with my own blood, and he'd nearly killed a woman tonight. Scum like this deserved to have his head smashed in with a fire extinguisher. Instead, I dragged him out of the bathroom. The angel in the other room had plans for him.

I continued to drag the vampire, making my way down the hall, wishing I were strong enough to throw him over my shoulder. But I wasn't, so I just kept pulling him along. Finally, I made it to the edge of the dance floor, where I deposited him next to his two buddies.

My angelic audience was waiting there, watching me struggle. In fact, he'd probably heard me struggling the whole time and hadn't lifted a finger to help.

"There were three vampires," I said. "You told me there was one."

"Yes, I did."

"That was a test?" I growled.

"In the Legion, you will often be put into unknown situations. You will have to adjust," he replied with calm indifference.

I glowered at him.

"There's no need for that," he said. "You managed adequately enough, though your methods were… unconventional."

"I told you I wasn't armed to take on vampires. In fact, I wasn't armed at all. You should be pleased by how well I adapted."

"You are indeed *scrappy*." He said the word as though he didn't know how he felt about it. "Is that from your time as a vagrant on the streets?"

I marched right up to him and stared him in the eye. "This is all a game to you, isn't it? Humans are just toys, props."

"It is our job to protect humans."

"But you don't really see us as the same as you, do you? I saw the cool way you looked at that woman, like you were healing her because it was what you were supposed to do. You don't care about us."

"If you'd seen what I have, you'd learn to stay detached," he said. "Too much death, too much pain. If you don't turn it off, you go mad. You will learn that."

"Never," I hissed. "Compassion is what separates men from monsters."

He looked down at me. "So you think I'm a monster?"

"Yes."

"Perhaps you're right," he allowed. "Perhaps, you can only survive the Legion if you lose a piece of your humanity. But *this* is what you're signing up for. Are you sure this is what you want?"

I saw Zane's face in my mind, as clearly as if he were

right in front of me. He needed me. He was counting on me to save him. I was the only one who could.

"Yes," I told the angel. "I am sure."

His voice dipped low, and I felt that same magic swirling around me, trying to mess with my head. "Why are you joining?"

I shook off his magic. It hurt when it broke against my skin, but I wouldn't let him see that. I kept my face hard, my tone cool as I said, "To save people. And I'll do it without losing who I am, without losing what makes me human."

He held my gaze for a moment longer, then he pulled out my application form. He set it down on the counter of the bar, signing it before handing the paper back to me.

"Congratulations, initiate. Welcome to the Legion of Angels."

"I'm in?"

"You're in," he confirmed. "Bring that form with you when you return to your new home in two hours."

Leaving me there at the bar, he headed back over the vampires. He tied them all together. With that done, he lifted them as one onto the counter, his muscles bulging under the combined weight of three vampires. Holy shit, he was strong. I began to turn away, to move toward the door, but his hand flashed out, catching mine.

"Leda Pierce, I will be watching you," he promised as six Legion soldiers marched into the bar to carry away the vampires.

CHAPTER SIX
The Last Day of My Life

TWO HOURS TO say goodbye to my old life. I almost wished the angel had made me stay in the Legion building until the blood-letting, collective torture, or whatever else the Legion had in store for me this afternoon. Staying would have made what was coming much easier.

But life was rarely easy and never fair. That's something I'd learned long before Calli had taken me in. I'd been making the tough choices for years already, but she'd taught me to make the *right* ones. And this was right. Saving the brother I loved was right. I knew in my heart that it was true.

It was nearly time for our return train to Purgatory to leave. I messaged Calli that I'd meet her and the girls at the station, then I headed there. The train was just pulling in as I arrived at the platform.

"Cutting it close, aren't you, Leda? What happened? Did you have a steamy rendezvous with a sexy man in the Armory?" Tessa smirked at me.

Not a man, an angel. And it wasn't in the Armory.

"Something happened. Just look at her face," Tessa said to Gin. "He must have been some guy."

"Not everything is about boys, Tessa," I replied.

"Of course it is, silly. You just haven't realized it yet."

Calli took my hands, looking me right in the eye. Her gaze slid over me like a search scope, her fingers tracing the scratches on my face, down to where the broken glass from the mirror had cut into my hands. "What happened? Were you attacked in the city?"

"I'm fine," I assured her. "It was just a few vampires."

Calli gave me a hard look. "What's going on here, Leda?"

"I'm not coming with you."

Calli stiffened, her grip on me tightening. I didn't trust myself to speak without my voice breaking, so I peeled her hands from mine, then reached into the back pocket of my jeans to recover the paper I'd received from the angel, the one accepting me into the Legion of Angels.

Calli's eyes widened as she read the text printed there. "Dear girl, what have you done?"

"What *had* to be done. You knew what Rose was saying as well as I. In order to save Zane, we first have to find him. We have no idea where he is. He's probably not even on Earth anymore. To find him, one of us must gain telepathic powers. And the only way to do that is to move up the Legion and earn that magic."

The Legion of Angels was structured into a rigid hierarchy. With every level you advanced up the ranks, you gained a new power.

"You sweet, foolish girl," Calli sighed. "That magic is a level nine spell, a second-tier angel spell. You not only have to make it through the ranks, you need to actually become an angel. Do you know how few people make it that far?"

"Very few," I said. "But I've never believed in being a victim to the odds."

"There's no going back now." Calli shook the paper. "They won't let you leave the Legion. Not ever."

"I know, and I'm sorry. I promised to help you with the business, and now I'm bailing. I just have to save Zane. I can't leave him at the mercy of the demons."

"I don't care about that silly promise I never wanted you to make. I care about *you*, Leda. One way or another, the Legion will claim your life. Even if your body survives, your soul does not. The Legion changes who you are inside."

"I will never change," I promised her, even as I couldn't help but think back to the angel's words, those words that echoed Calli's. But just because he'd changed, that didn't mean I would. I had to believe that.

"It's the only way, Mom," I said, tears burning my eyes, blurring my vision. "The only way to connect to Zane. And only I can do it."

"No," Tessa's voice cut in, sharp as a whip. "You could have told us. We could have decided together who joined the Legion." Enormous tears rolled down her cheeks, which only made it harder for me to hold back my own tears.

"You and Gin can't do it," I told her. "The Legion only accepts initiates after they turn twenty-two."

"We could have lied," Gin said. She and Tessa were holding to each other, wailing. "We have fake ids."

"That works on bartenders, little sister, *not* on the Legion."

Calli's mouth tightened into a hard line. "Leda, what's our number one rule?"

"We always stick together," I said automatically, then sighed. "But things are different now. We aren't all together. We won't be until after we get Zane back."

"We'll never be together again, even if you save Zane.

Because the Legion won't let you leave," Gin sobbed.

I smiled sadly at her. "A small price to pay to save our brother from being exploited. You know what the demons will do to him. They'll crush his mind, making him spy on their enemies until he burns out—or goes mad." And, if Rose was right, they'd also try to breed him to make more ghosts. Like an animal. I shuddered at the thought.

"Many of the Legion's initiates don't survive the first cut," Calli told me. "The flood of magic kills them outright."

"I'm too stubborn to die."

Her eyes were as hard as diamonds, her stance as unmovable as a boulder. She'd used this attack before, mostly back when I'd been a teenager. I'd backed down more than a few times because of it—but I wasn't backing down this time.

"If I die, Zane is lost to us," I said. "That's enough to keep me fighting."

Calli swept me into a hug. "You are a foolish girl," she said against my cheek. "You have a big heart, but you could still learn a thing or two about using your head. Why didn't you talk to us first? We always make decisions together."

"Not this time," I said. "You would have tried to talk me out of it. Or you'd have signed up with the Legion yourself. *That* would have been truly foolish."

The Legion had a minimum age but no maximum age. And I saw it in Calli's eyes now that she would have enlisted herself to keep me out. She'd have signed her own death sentence by joining. As good as she was, she couldn't keep up with the younger initiates. And her magic wasn't as malleable. The infusion of magic would have killed her, no matter what she thought.

"I know you think I'm crazy, but I've thought

everything through, and I'm the best chance we've got," I told her. "Gin and Tessa are too young, and Bella is too gentle for the Legion. They would eat her alive. She wouldn't make it through the Legion. And neither would you, Calli. I'm the only one of us who even has a chance."

The train expelled a loud cloud of steam.

"Go," I said, nudging them toward their ride home. "You have to go."

"Come with us," Gin pleaded.

"She can't now," said Tessa. "The Legion took her. She can't run. They'd chase her."

I smiled at them all. "Go. I'll be fine. I'll write to you whenever I can. And send you treats from the city."

"Leda," Calli began, then stopped.

"Don't worry about me. I'm a survivor."

"You always have been," Calli said, resting her hand on my cheek.

The train whistled again, and she turned, hurrying my crying sisters toward the nearest carriage. They went inside and, as the train began to pull out of the station, they took their seats at the window. I stood there and watched until the train was out of sight. Then I wiped the tears from my eyes and turned to face my new life.

◈ ◇ ◈ ◇ ◈

I walked back to the Legion building. I had over an hour before I needed to be back there, but I saw no reason to dawdle. There was a bimonthly orientation for all new Legion initiates, every two months, always on the first of the month. That was today. That was a small sliver of luck in a wretched situation. The sooner I got this over with, the sooner I'd be on my way to saving Zane. It was time to embrace my fate.

When I arrived, one of the Legion soldiers, a woman who looked only a few years older than I was, was waiting. She had the insignia of a hand on the jacket of her feminine suit. She showed me into the back. This time, we walked all the way to the end of the hallway of closed rooms, then pushed through another set of double doors to enter a grand ballroom where twenty other initiates waited. I could tell they were initiates from the lack of Legion insignia on their clothes—and from the anxiety hanging over them like a storm cloud.

Even more opulent than the entrance hall at the witches' university, the enormous ballroom was pure decadence at its finest. The floors were cherrywood, and the walls were painted in the most elaborate and vibrant scene of angels I'd seen yet. Three long buffet tables covered in overflowing floral arrangements, very posh finger foods, and tiny glass shot glasses of juice sat against one wall. It looked like we were here for a posh cocktail hour, not down and dirty paranormal bootcamp. I didn't know what I'd been expecting, but it sure wasn't this. I was really underdressed for this opulent affair. Thankfully, so were most of the other initiates.

Most, but not all. The doors burst open, and eight men and women strode into the ballroom like they owned it. Like the other initiates, they were also wearing denim and leather, but it was all designer-made and really expensive. As I ventured closer to the ground they'd claimed around the cheese spread and wine, I understood how they could each afford an outfit it would have taken me a month to save up for. They were all exchanging stories about their parents. Every single one of them apparently had an angel for a mother or father.

As I listened to them brag about all the heroic things their parents had done, two initiates joined me beside the fruit bowl. The woman was about my height and as willowy as a model. With her perfect complexion, slender figure, and hair that flowed like a crimson waterfall, she looked like she belonged on a runway—not ready to take the plunge to join an elite military legion that might very well kill her. The man beside her was a head taller than the both of us and built like a football player. Amusement curled his lips. He was clearly the sort of person who could find the humor in any moment, no matter how dire.

"Legion brats." The woman rolled her eyes at the group of angel spawn. "They think they know everything." She looked me over and declared, "You seem normal."

"I guess that's a matter of opinion," I replied.

The woman laughed. It was a friendly, genuine laugh, and it made me like her immediately. "Ain't that the truth?" She extended her hand to me. "I'm Ivy."

I shook her hand. "Leda."

"And I'm Drake. So lovely to meet you, Leda." The man took my hand, kissing the top of it.

Ivy elbowed him in the side. "You'll have to excuse Drake. He fancies himself a prince."

"Or an angel?" I asked, arching my brows.

Drake grinned at me. "We all have to aim high."

"First, we have to make it through the initiation ceremony," said Ivy.

I dropped my voice. "What can you tell me about it?"

"No one knows." Ivy smirked at the brats. "For all their flair and show, they don't know any more than we do. Even though they pretend that they do. The Legion keeps everything super secret. Speaking of the rituals is strictly forbidden. Their parents wouldn't tell them. The Legion treats information leaks like a virus." She pounded her fist against her palm. "They annihilate them."

"Why did you join?" I asked them.

"Drake and I have known each other for forever basically," Ivy said. "Or at least since we were babies. Our mothers are best friends. They even gave birth on the same day. So Drake and I grew up as best friends. We've hardly ever been apart." Her cheerful facade slipped. She teared up as she looked at her friend.

"What is it?" I asked.

Drake took Ivy's hand. "Ivy's mother is dying of cancer. There's nothing any magic or medicine can do for her."

"I'm so sorry."

Ivy wiped the tears from her eyes and put on a brave smile. "Don't be. It will soon be over either way."

"The witches' magic can't help her, her pleas to the Legion for healing have gone unanswered, but if she can reach the seventh level of the Legion, she can save her mother with fairy magic," Drake said.

"I only hope I survive and can make it to that level before the cancer kills her."

"Why doesn't your mother petition to be turned into a vampire?" I asked. "That would heal her."

"Been there, done that," said Ivy. "Or tried to anyway. The list to become a vampire is a mile long. The only way to make it to the top is to know someone on the inside." She sighed. "Which we don't. Oddly enough, the list to join the Legion is never long."

Because they kept crossing names off of that list. When the initiates died. No, I couldn't think like that. I had to believe I would make it. I was Zane's only hope.

So I put on a smile and looked at Drake. "You're a good friend to come with Ivy so she doesn't have to do this alone."

"Nah, I told you. I want to become an angel to get the ladies." He laughed, but the way he was standing over Ivy's shoulder spoke for itself. He would protect her with everything he had.

Ivy laughed. "Is that what you put on your application form?" she asked her friend.

"Of course." He mussed up his short black hair with a smile. "It's not like they ever reject anyone. They figure if you're weak or crazy, you'll end up dead and not be their problem anymore."

"Why are you here?" Ivy asked me.

I liked Ivy and Drake, but I couldn't tell them. The truth about Zane had to remain a secret. From everyone, friend or not.

"To stop rampaging supernaturals from hurting people," I said.

Ivy laughed. "Good old number one. That answer has been written so many times into application forms that it's practically stenciled into the clipboards. I can't believe they actually believed you."

"They didn't," I told her. "The guy who interviewed me basically told me I was full of shit."

Drake snorted.

"Yeah, they like to cut through the crap here," said Ivy.

Drake nodded in agreement. I was grateful that they didn't pry any further into my reasons for being here. They seemed to understand that I didn't want to share them.

"Still, Leda, you should tread carefully," Drake warned me. "The Legion doesn't like secrets. They demand our total obedience, secrets and all. If you provoke them, they will push harder."

"So I guess it wasn't a good idea to mouth off to the

angel who interviewed me?" I commented.

Their mouths dropped.

"What? That bad?" I bit my lip. "I was nervous. When I get nervous, my mouth runs away with me."

"An *angel* interviewed you?" Ivy said in obvious shock.

"Yeah."

Drake was shaking his head in disbelief.

"Is that bad?"

"Well, it's either very good or very bad," Drake said. "But since this is the Legion, I'm going to go with very bad."

"Why?"

"Because angels don't interview initiates. Like ever," he told me. "It's beneath them. You must have done something to catch someone's attention."

"I didn't do anything. I just filled out the form, then went to that room. Maybe I mouthed off a little, but that was after the angel came in. I was a model initiate before that."

Ivy gave me a wry look.

I sighed. "Ok, maybe only ninety percent model initiate. I think we're just blowing this out of proportion." I hoped. I did not need to have the Legion watching my every move. "What did you two have to do for your interview?"

They looked confused.

"Uh, what?" Drake asked.

"What task did you have to do for your interview?" I clarified.

He and Ivy exchanged loaded looks, then Ivy said, "We didn't do anything. We just filled out the forms, and the guy signed them. He was some low-level Legion guy. He looked bored and like he just wanted to get out of there and make it back to the break room before all the donuts were gone."

"Why do you ask? Did you have to do something?" Drake asked me.

"The angel brought me to a bar and had me apprehend three vampires."

Ivy blinked in surprise. "Whoa."

"And you survived?" Drake said, looking me over as though he didn't believe I was really standing there talking to them.

"The vampires were new and drunk and kind of stupid. Luckily for me. The last vampire I took on was worse than those three put together."

Ivy gaped at me.

Drake chuckled. "What did you do for a living? Before you decided to join the gods' army, that is?"

"Bounty hunter," I replied.

He whistled, low and long. "Paranormal bounty hunter."

"I tried to steer clear of most supernatural jobs. The payout isn't worth the high chance of death," I told him. "That vampire slipped through the cracks. Whoever posted his bounty neglected to mention that he wasn't human."

"That bites," Drake said.

"Tell me about it. Have either of you ever fought supernaturals?"

"I haven't fought anything more sentient than a dust bunny," Ivy said.

"I don't know. Some of those dust bunnies seem to have a mind of their own." Drake looked fondly at his best friend. "Ivy doesn't fight crime, but she was a killer cheerleader. Those backflips and side kicks were pretty wicked."

Ivy grinned back at him. "Not as wicked as your football skills."

"Yeah, I'm sure the ability to toss a ball around a field will come in handy against monsters," someone laughed loudly.

Eight someones actually. The Legion brats were striding over, belligerent sneers on their faces. This wasn't going to end well.

"What do you call it when a cheerleader, a jock, and a small town bounty hunter join the Legion of Angels?" one of them asked the others. "A triple suicide."

They all burst into laughter. Ivy clenched her fists. Drake set his hand on her shoulder, holding her back. The Legion brats continued to laugh.

"You need to work on your jokes," I told them, channeling serenity. "That wasn't even funny."

"Actually, it was *very* funny."

"I thought it was funny, Dallas," one of the Legion brats told him.

"Give up now, children," Dallas said with a disparaging smile. "You're as good as dead."

"Yeah, well at least Leda made it through an interview. I bet you didn't," Ivy shot back.

"Of course not. *We* are descended from angels. We're assured entry. We don't need an interview. But I'm glad the Legion is starting to implement them for the lesser folk. Maybe it will keep out all the riffraff who believe themselves worthy of joining."

The rest of them laughed in agreement. I'd never put up with bullies in high school, and my tolerance for them hadn't improved since. But my response was cut short when the woman who'd shown me here rang the bell sitting on the podium at the center of the ballroom.

"Good afternoon, initiates." She looked around at everyone in the ballroom. Since I'd arrived, our numbers had swelled to fifty. "I am Captain Basanti Somerset. You have come here today to join the ranks of the Legion of Angels. You are about to embark on a journey few others on this Earth will ever take, a journey that will require you to be brave, intelligent, and to push your body and mind beyond the breaking point. It is a great responsibility, but the rewards are just as great. If you have what it takes."

In front of me, the Legion brats were grinning at one another.

"And now allow me to introduce your commanding officer for this training," Captain Somerset said. "Colonel Nero Windstriker."

Awed whispers rippled across the crowd of initiates as an angel in a black leather suit strode across the ballroom to join the captain at the podium. I held back a gasp as I recognized the angel who'd interrogated me just a few hours ago. This time, he had his wings out. A mix of blue and green and black feathers, they nearly kissed the ground as he walked.

They were the most beautiful thing I'd ever seen. His wings shimmered with an ethereal light that delighted my senses, penetrating me to my very soul. I couldn't look away, even as his emerald eyes met mine with a look that was no less penetrating. Several of the women gasped at the angel as he passed. Some of the men too.

Nero stopped beside the podium. "Welcome to the last day of your life." He paused a moment to let us take that in. "From here on out, your life belongs to the Legion. Your mind, your magic, your body, your soul—they all belong to us." His gaze slid across the group of initiates, landing on me. "You have signed up to serve a higher purpose. To uphold the laws of the gods, to fight the monsters who would tear this world apart, to protect the innocent and the weak. To do this, the Legion will grant you powers. You will grow faster. Stronger. Smarter. You will have the power to enchant. To heal. To control the very elements themselves. You will come to possess magic that others can only dream of. The higher you climb in the Legion, the more powers you will gain.

"But it will come at a price. Power always comes at a price. Many of you will not survive. Those of you who do live will shed your humanity altogether. You will become something else." He lifted his hands into the air, his wings spreading wide. "Are you ready?"

The Legion brats lifted up their hands. Others in the room followed, caught up in the magic of his speech.

I could feel Nero's enchantment winding through the room. He was riling them up, making them want to follow where he led. This was how the angels commanded armies. Beside me, Ivy and Drake lifted up their hands too. Everyone's hands were in the air.

Except mine.

Nero's eyes locked onto me, watching me with an intensity I could hardly bear. It took every shred of willpower to fight the magic he was casting around me, to keep control of my mind. Sweat dribbled down my neck, but I held on. I gave the angel a small smirk—I just couldn't help it, even knowing that it would cost me later, that he'd realize his siren's song didn't work on me—but I lifted my hand too, slowly and of my own free will.

Nero held my gaze for a few moments, then he addressed the crowd. "The time has come."

He indicated the fountain beside him. It began gurgling and bubbling a crimson liquid. Some kind of juice? Except it had an unnatural gleam to it. Magic. The longer I looked at it, the more I realized it bore an unfortunate resemblance to blood.

I obviously wasn't the only one thinking that. The other initiates held back, clearly wanting nothing to do with that creepy fountain.

Except for the Legion brats. They marched up to the fountain with complete confidence, their ringleader Dallas at the front. Nero dipped a golden goblet into the pool of crimson liquid, then handed it to him. Dallas drank it down in a single gulp, smiling widely. The first convulsion knocked the goblet from his hand. The second knocked him to the ground, where he lay, spasming and seizing as whatever he'd drunk slowly killed him.

CHAPTER SEVEN
First Sip

WITH A CRISP flick of Nero's wrist, one of the Legion soldiers standing around the room moved in and carried the convulsing initiate away. The other Legion brats clustered together, the arrogance wiped from their faces. They seemed to have realized that if their ringleader could fall, so could any of them. The realization hit them hard. At least half of them looked like they were going to puke.

Nero turned to the room of initiates and said coolly, "Next."

"What is in that goblet?" someone asked.

"Next," Nero repeated.

The initiates exchanged nervous glances.

"Will he live?" one of the Legion brats asked.

"For a time," said Nero. "What's in that fountain will either kill you or make you stronger. The end result is entirely up to you."

No one was moving a muscle.

"I'll go," I declared, my voice echoing through the ballroom.

It sounded so sure, so confident. So completely unlike everything I was feeling right now.

"You're really brave," Ivy whispered to me.

"No," I told her. "I just don't believe in putting off the inevitable." With every passing second, my stomach was twisting up into an even tighter knot. If I didn't do this now, I'd never be able to do it.

Nero motioned me forward. As I walked toward the fountain, all eyes were glued on me. The distance felt immense, and I held the angel's gaze the whole time. His expression was unreadable. Like granite. No, marble. Cold, smooth, and not an emotion etched into it.

Nero handed me the golden goblet. My hand shook as I dipped it into the strange fluid, so I steadied it with the other. And then, taking a deep breath, I drank.

It didn't taste like blood. An explosion of flavors tickled my tongue. It was sweet, by far the sweetest thing I'd ever tasted, but there was something else. My other senses were being bombarded with a whirlwind of sounds and sights and smells. Overcome with dizziness, I stumbled to the side. Nero's hands flashed out, catching me. But before I could meet his eyes, he nudged me aside.

"Come on, initiates," he said, loud and clear. "Form a line."

As they marched to the fountain, single file and solemn, I leaned against the wall. Everything was zipping past me at five hundred miles per hour. My body rocked and then stumbled again, and I threw up everything in my stomach all over the floor. Wiping my mouth, I straightened and looked across the ballroom. The other initiates were shaking. Some were dying on the floor, convulsing even more wildly than Dallas had. A man near the back of the line gaped at the men and women on the floor—then he turned and ran.

He didn't make it far. As he fled, one of the Legion

soldiers pulled out her gun and shot him in the back of the head.

A hand touched down on my shoulder, and I turned to find Nero there, holding the goblet out to me.

"Drink," he said.

"I did."

"You threw it up before it could enter your bloodstream."

He sounded like he was chastising me. Like it was my fault that I'd thrown it up.

I looked down at the man with a bullet through his head. "Did you have to shoot him?"

"He signed up for this. He chose to be here. Once you join, there is no leaving. One or two always try to run once they see what's happening."

His cold tone chilled me to my bones, even though I should have known better. After all, I'd been the one to tell him he'd lost part of his humanity.

As Nero set the full goblet into my hands, magic buzzed across his skin onto mine. It was an oddly enjoyable feeling, so much so that I was almost tempted to brush my hand against his again to repeat the sensation. Whatever magic had passed between us, it hadn't been one way. Surprise flashed across Nero's face before he quickly cooled his expression.

I lifted the goblet to my lips and drank. This time, the liquid went down more easily. My hands shook as I lowered the goblet from my mouth, but I managed to keep upright this time—and not throw up on his shoes.

"You're stronger than you look," he told me.

I allowed a small smile to touch my lips. "I know you didn't mean that as a compliment, but I'm going to take it that way."

"It's a fact. You look so…soft."

"Well, I'm tough."

"Yes," he agreed, taking the goblet back.

I suppressed a shiver when his hand briefly brushed against mine, igniting my skin with a rush of magic that felt better than I wanted to admit to myself. I had the odd feeling that he'd done that on purpose, but I couldn't fathom why. Maybe he was testing me.

Nero set the goblet down on the edge of the fountain, then turned to address the twenty-four of us who remained. Twenty-four out of fifty. That was just insane. I scanned the crowd quickly for Ivy and Drake. Relief flooded me when I saw that they were among the survivors.

"Captain Somerset will show you to the barracks," Nero declared. "Change and then report to Hall 3. You have fifteen minutes."

The Legion brats followed right behind Captain Somerset. Six of them had survived out of eight. It appeared that having an angel for a parent significantly increased your chances of surviving whatever magic was in that fountain. The Legion brats chatted merrily along, as though two of their own hadn't just dropped dead in front of them. I had a feeling that it was precisely this total lack of humanity that the Legion was looking for in its soldiers. Maybe this had all been a huge mistake.

But I kept walking, one foot in front of the other. I'd set down this path, and I was going to finish it. I was going to find my brother.

We followed Captain Somerset down the bright and shiny hallway. There were four rooms here, each one with six beds. The Legion brats immediately claimed one of the rooms for themselves. The rest of us divided up between the three remaining rooms. Captain Somerset left us to it.

"Not much for privacy, are they?" Ivy commented as she, Drake, and I claimed a room along with three other women.

I took a stack of neatly folded sports clothes from the shared dresser that barely fit between the beds. "Apparently not."

I'd changed clothes with my sisters around and even my brother, but this was different. These people were strangers. On the other hand, changing in the open was the least of the problems we'd soon face.

"We have to hurry," Ivy said, pulling off her shirt. "If you're late, then Colonel Sexy Angel might march up and give you his piecing stare."

"Colonel Sexy Angel?" Drake asked, amused.

He had the decency not to gawk at the half-naked women around him, but not all of them were returning the favor. He didn't seem to mind, though. On the contrary, he was clearly basking in the attention. He shot one of our new roommates a wink, and she hastily looked away, giggling.

"Yes, Colonel Sexy Angel," Ivy said. "At least the cloud of impending doom hanging over our heads will be a tad sweeter with him around. Yum."

The other women expressed their enthusiastic agreement.

"I wouldn't mind having him spank me," one said.

Everyone nodded, except for me and Drake. He just rolled his eyes.

"What do you think, girl?" Ivy asked me as she slid on her sports tights.

"About what?" I asked, fastening the sports bra that had come with my new Legion clothing set.

"About Nero Windstriker, of course. Back in the

ballroom, he was giving you a smoldering stare the whole time." Ivy sighed.

"Yeah, he thinks I'm hiding something."

Ivy twisted her hair up into a high ponytail. "Everyone is hiding something."

"Ivy, that's not how angels think," Drake told her. "To them, secrets are meant to be exposed, minds cracked…"

"Bones broken," I finished bleakly.

But Drake just grinned. "Precisely. Angels are the knights of justice, the voice of the gods. They always get what they want."

Ivy tossed him his pile of sports clothes. "Less talking, more changing. I don't think you would enjoy it as much as we would if Colonel Sexy Angel spanked you."

Everyone laughed.

"But he's actually right," one of our roommates said, looking at me. "If Nero Windstriker has decided he will find out what you're hiding, he will find out what you're hiding. You might as well go to him now and confess your sins."

The woman next to her slouched over. "They will break us."

I tried not to think about it. I had to stay focused on my goal: to make it through the ranks, to get strong. And to do it without letting anyone find out about Zane's powers.

"Don't listen to them," Ivy whispered to me.

I smiled at her. "Of course not. Let's make a pact, you and I. A pact that we won't break."

"You got it, sister."

But past the tough face I put on for the world, I was cold on the inside. The twenty-six people who had died today hadn't even had a chance. One moment they'd been alive, and the next they weren't. And they wouldn't be the first to die. The culling ceremony was complete, but this was far from over.

CHAPTER EIGHT
What Doesn't Kill You...

WE WERE ALL changed and ready to go when Captain Somerset returned to show us to Hall 3, which meant we could hopefully forego all spankings. But as I'd soon experience firsthand, there was more than one way to torture an initiate. In fact, there were endless ways.

Hall 3 was a big gym with an obstacle course of barriers and structures at its core. A full-sized track looped around that core, and beyond it lay climbing walls and other obstacle courses. Nero stood with another member of the Legion, a man with cropped blond hair and a relaxed, good-natured smile. Each of them was wearing an athletic suit that drew more than a few whispers of appreciation from my fellow female initiates.

"This is Major Harker Locke," Nero said, his voice piercing the whispering crowd. "He will be assisting me with your training."

The major gave us a wave too friendly to have come from a member of the Legion.

"Now let's get down to business," Nero continued. "This begins the first stage of your training. You must now train your bodies and minds, to prove that you are truly one of us."

"Aren't we already in?" someone asked.

"No." The word punched through the crowd gathered before him.

"But we took your test and survived."

"You survived your first sip of the Nectar of the Gods," Nero replied. "The drink that sparked your magic, bringing to the surface what was hidden inside of you. But it remains to be seen if you have what it takes to join the Legion of Angels. If you do, you will drink from the gods' cup once more to receive their first gift: Vampire's Kiss. It will give you strength, speed, stamina, and self-healing—all the powers of a vampire. You will gain the ability to receive a boost in those powers when you consume the lifeblood of another."

The initiates around me began buzzing with excitement.

"But beware," said Nero, his words silencing the crowd. "Along with these new powers comes also the other side of vampires: the hunger. You must learn to control it, not let the hunger control you. Become a master of the hunger, the bloodlust, the magic. Otherwise, you will go wild, turning into a monster. And you will be put down." He tapped the gun at his side. "This magic will either kill you, or it will make you stronger. Remember that, initiates: what doesn't kill you only makes you stronger."

Or what doesn't kill you just kills you later, I thought.

"Whether you live or die is entirely up to you. We will work on your strength, stamina, and willpower to give you a chance of surviving the Nectar. We start now." Nero pointed to the track. "Ten laps. Go."

After our ten laps, Nero had us do pushups until we dropped. Then he made us run another ten laps. Rinse and repeat into infinity. He pushed us until our bodies shook and spasmed and we collapsed to the ground. Then he made us go again. And the fun was only just beginning.

"Gather round," Nero said as my heart made a solid effort of exploding through my chest.

From the looks of my fellow initiates sprawled across the ground all around me, they'd fared the past few hours no better. But we peeled our bodies from the floor and walked over to him.

"Many of you will not survive the first month," Nero declared, not even a hint of sympathy staining his perfect face as his eyes panned across us. The angel was as soulless as he was beautiful.

"As I said before, we will try to prepare you as best we can," he continued. "But in the end, whether or not you survive the gods' first gift is entirely in your hands. This is as much a physical battle as it is a mental one. And that is what we will train now."

"Now? What was all that we just did?" someone asked.

"Warmup," Nero replied coolly.

We followed him across the gym and into a smaller room. At the end of that room, a door waited. Splashes of crimson stained its steel surface. Blood. It was blood.

"Who can tell me what this is?" Nero asked us, tapping the door.

I couldn't stop staring at the blood—or dreading whatever was coming next.

"A blast door. It's designed to resist the force of an explosion," one of the initiates said immediately. He had an ashen face, pale nearly to the point of sickly. He was built like a rail, all skin and bones with hardly any muscle. It was a wonder he hadn't passed out during our previous exercises. Then again, you couldn't always tell how strong someone was from their outward appearance.

"Yes," Nero said to him, then addressed us all. "This represents a formidable opponent. You cannot break it. You cannot defeat it."

"It's just a door," someone whispered behind me.

Nero's eyes darted to the whisperer. "This isn't just a door. This is *you*. Your greatest enemy. This is what stands in your way." He motioned the whisperer forward.

The man came, a half-smirk on his face. Nero's next words wiped that smirk away.

"Punch the door," he told the initiate.

"Like for real?"

"You will put your full power into that punch to hit the door as hard as you can," said Nero. "And then you will immediately punch it again."

A slow smile began to creep up the whisperer's lips, but the cold look in Nero's eyes killed it. The whisperer's eyes darted between Nero and the door.

"Now, initiate," Nero told him in a voice that made goosebumps pop up all across my skin.

The whisperer swallowed hard, then punched the door.

"I said to use your *full* power," Nero said, his face as hard as granite, his eyes as cold as an Arctic storm.

"But that will break my hand," the whisperer protested.

"Keep your wrist straight."

"It will still hurt."

"That's the point. What will you do the first time the enemy hits you?"

The whisperer's mouth dropped. "I… Is this some sort of punishment?"

"This is the exercise I have ordered you to complete," said Nero.

No one asked what would happen if we disobeyed. I

didn't think anyone wanted to know. The whisperer stared at the door for a second, then his body wound up, throwing a hard punch at the door. His shriek of pure agony wailed over the steel echoes. He dropped to his knees, cradling his broken and bleeding hand. Nero looked down at him, his face impassive, unfeeling.

"I told you to keep your wrist straight. Harker, take a look at his hand."

As the major healed the whisperer with his magic touch, Nero scanned the initiates for his next victim.

"You," he said, his eyes settling on Drake. "The football player. Let's see if you punch better than the truck driver."

Drake broke away from us and marched up to the door and punched it with so much force that the echoes nearly shook the walls. Drake bit down on his lip, containing whatever agony was boiling inside of him.

"Again," Nero said, the word cracking like a whip.

Drake looked down at his hand. It didn't appear to be broken, but it was bleeding.

"Again."

Drake wound up his fist for the punch—then dropped his hand.

"Your willpower is lacking," Nero said, dismissing Drake with a crisp flick of his wrist.

The angel summoned us one by one to that damn door until, finally, I was the only one left. I didn't think this was by accident. He'd given me a front row seat to the pain of all twenty-three initiates that had come before me, and now it was my turn. As I strode toward that door, his eyes followed me, boring into me like a drill that could penetrate my body, cutting through to my raw soul. I turned my gaze from him and stared down that door. Then, before my mind could flinch away from the reality of what

I was about to do, I hit it as hard as I could.

Agony exploded on my fist, rushing like a burning river through my nerves, up my arms. Surprise mixed with the pain—surprise that I could even hit hard enough to nearly break my arm. Grinding my teeth against the welling pain, I slammed my fist into the door a second time. My bleeding knuckles scraped against steel, dousing the fire with lighter fluid. I turned and faced down the sadistic angel.

His gaze dipped briefly to the blood dripping from my quaking hands. "You need to work on your form," he said.

Screw you, I mentally shot him.

His mouth tightened, as though he'd heard me. Maybe he had. An angel of his level had telepathic powers. Just in case he was tuned in to my thoughts, I shot him an image of me setting his wings on fire with a flamethrower. If he'd read my thoughts, he didn't betray any hint of emotion.

"You must go into any battle expecting to get hurt," he said to us all. "And you must learn to plow through the pain. If not, you will die. There are no timeouts on the battlefield—or from the magic that will rip through your body when you drink again of the gods' Nectar. If your will is not strong enough, you *will* die. There are no quitters here, only soldiers of the Legion and the dead. Remember that the next time you think you can just give up."

A few of the initiates shifted their weight uncomfortably.

Nero indicated the blood-stained door. "This was an exercise in willpower, in holding yourself together despite great pain. And you failed spectacularly," he declared. "Except one of you." He turned to find me. "Congratulations, Leda Pierce, you've advanced to the next level."

Why did that sound more like a punishment than a reward?

Nero flicked his hand at the blast door. It responded to his magic, swinging open, and a wolfish dog bounded out, baring his hellish teeth.

"And now you will fight," Nero told me.

CHAPTER NINE
The Torturer of Desperate Souls

THE DOG DARTED forward, snapping its teeth at me. I moved aside, my leg barely avoiding impalement on its mouth of daggers. Quick as lightning, it moved again—and this time, I wasn't so lucky. Pain ruptured my thigh, pouring down my leg like a bloody waterfall. I stumbled back, trying to get away from the beast.

It was waiting for me.

It launched onto its back legs and bit me in the shoulder. Its pointed jaws clamped on tight, pulling me down to the ground. Its third bite pierced my calf.

"You must conquer the pain and fight through it," Nero's voice said through the haze clouding my mind.

Black spots danced across my eyes. I clenched my teeth and tried to remain conscious. The dog was a big blurry blotch somewhere near my foot. I kicked at it. I must have hit its nose because it yelped in pain and retreated a step. This was my chance. I tried to use that moment to stand, but my body refused to move. And the moment was too brief. The dog snapped at me again and again. The pain melted together into one solid stream of agony. Numbness followed, and then darkness.

When I came to, Harker was standing over me, his hand on my leg. A golden glow pulsed out from his hand, spreading in gentle, humming waves across my skin. My wounds sealed, and my head cleared enough to see Nero standing a few steps away, the dog sitting by his side. The beast's eyes were dancing about wildly, like it wanted to finish what it had started, but whatever spell Nero had cast over it was keeping it in place.

"Are you all right?" Harker asked me, smiling with encouragement as he moved his hand from my leg to my arm.

I forced a smile to my aching lips. Everything in my body ached, though that feeling was fading fast. In a few seconds, I might even feel human again instead of like some dog's chew toy.

"I'm fine," I told Harker, allowing him to help me to my feet.

He shot me a little wink, then went to stand beside Nero. The dog was walking back to the blast door. As soon as it was standing on the other side, the steel slab slammed shut behind it.

"You will need to practice that again," Nero said.

"Again?" I replied, horrified. The memory of that beast's jaw cutting through my body sent shivers down my spine. "I have to do that again?"

He stepped toward me. "You will have to do this and more every day."

He reached out to me. I tried to pull away, but he was quicker. His hand closed around my wrist. As his other hand brushed across my skin, pain bubbled up.

"You missed a spot," he told Harker.

A smile touched Harker's lips. "So I did."

Nero's fingertip glowed, golden and blinding. He

tapped it to the cut in my arm. A rush of warmth cascaded through my body, pulsing in time to my heartbeat in a beautiful, intoxicating melody of magic. I inhaled deeply, drawing the delicious scent of that magic into me.

"Why are you here?" he asked, his voice dancing on the notes of the sweet song swirling inside my head.

I opened my mouth to tell him everything, to spill every secret I had. They were his to have. Every single one of them.

I stopped. What was I saying? I couldn't tell him anything. He was an angel. And he was working his magic on me. I pushed away from him, and he didn't try to stop me. He just watched me as the last of his magical song faded out of my head. A sense of profound loss cut through my previous contentment, leaving me shivering and sad. I wanted to feel his magic again, even knowing it wasn't real. None of this was real. This was a game he was playing, an angel's game. I took another step away from him. I would *not* let him have that power over me.

Surprise flashed in his emerald eyes. Maybe no one had ever resisted his siren's song before. But that breath of surprise quickly hardened into granite as he turned to address all of the initiates.

"You will train willpower here," he said. "You must resist pain and fear and any enemy you might face in battle. But you must never resist those who command you."

Even though his eyes scanned the crowd of initiates, I could feel them on me.

"The Legion has no use for soldiers who question orders. We need to know that in battle you will listen to your superiors, that you will do what you're told. No fear. No hesitation. No questioning." His eyes fell on me. "You can either obey me by choice, or I will make you obey."

A wave of pure power shot out from him. All around me, my fellow initiates began falling to their knees. Nero's magic tore at me, fierce this time rather than sweet. The sheer power of his magic felt like a mountain on my shoulders, pressing me down inch by inch. It *hurt* to resist—hurt more than punching that door, more than the dog mauling me—but every fiber of my being rebelled against his control.

You shouldn't resist, a voice said inside my head. It didn't sound like Nero's voice. It sounded like my own.

And the voice, that sensible part of me, was right. I shouldn't resist. I had to behave. I was here to gain the power I needed to save my brother, not to prove that I could stand up to an angel. So I stopped fighting. Relief flooded me immediately—relief from the agony of that heavy weight on my shoulders, relief from thinking. It was so easy to obey, to let someone make the decisions for me. A warm blanket of magic enveloped us all, protecting us, leading us. Uniting us.

"Obedience is everything," Nero said. A halo shining like a million crushed diamonds lit up his body. "You can hate me all you want, but you will follow my orders. Do you understand?"

We all nodded, unable to speak.

"Good," he said, releasing his hold on us. As the layers of his spell dissolved into the air, the easy contentment I'd felt faded away. "Now stand up, initiates, and run another ten laps."

◈ ◇ ◈ ◇ ◈

The next few weeks passed in a repeating loop of agony. Nero had us run until we couldn't stand, do pushups until our arms gave out, and punch that cursed door over and over again until our blood stained it too. We jumped from great heights and ran through obstacle courses designed to break our bodies. And we did this often after only two hours of sleep. Sleep deprivation was one of Nero's favorite tools.

We had to fight dogs—and then one another with swords, knives, and all kinds of other weapons from the Legion's arsenal. Bleeding was no excuse for giving up and neither were missing limbs. Nero pointed out that he could heal our wounds after the fight. If we fought well and didn't surrender, he even did that right away. If we didn't…well, he waited longer to heal us.

The man was a twisted, sadistic beast, and before the end of the first week, I wanted to kill him. By the end of the second week, I'd decided that death was too good for him. I had to make him suffer first.

By the end of the first month, I was too exhausted to fantasize about killing him. The only thing that kept me going was my need to save my brother.

"Pick up the pace, Pandora," Nero called out.

Pandora was his nickname for me. Apparently, our first conversation had left an impression, the one where I'd talked about my family's business Pandora's Box. So I was the bringer of evil and chaos? Well, it was better than being the torturer of desperate souls.

That was Nero's job. It was almost the end of the day, and my body was shaking. I was only halfway to the top of the climbing wall, and I was desperately pleading with my muscles not to collapse. Of course Nero had left the climbing wall for the end of the obstacle course from hell, when everyone was twenty shades past exhaustion and failure meant falling twenty feet. And there wasn't even a safety net. Apparently, that would be cheating because there were no safety nets in life. I guess I should have been happy the angel hadn't placed spikes at the bottom.

I muttered a few choice curses under my breath.

"Less cursing my existence and those that bore me into this world, and more climbing, initiate," Nero called up at me. "This climb is on a timer, and if that time runs out, I'll come up there and throw your ass down."

I cursed him some more, but I kept climbing, pushing myself harder. I was not going to give him the satisfaction of seeing me fall to my death. I made it to the top and hit the buzzer button.

"Thirty-one seconds to go," Nero said. "Cutting it a bit close, aren't you, initiate?"

I threw a look of pure loathing down at him, but I didn't think he even saw it. He was already busy harassing the next initiate trying to make her way up the wall. I descended slowly, trying to get back to solid ground without falling. As soon as I touched down, I headed straight for the water pitcher.

"Four more laps," Nero told me as the cool water touched my lips. "And another four for drinking without permission."

My feet felt like lead, but I gulped down the rest of the water in my cup, then took off running down the track. Ahead of me, I saw Ivy stumble and fall. I hurried over to her, trying to help her to her feet. But my friend just shook and heaved in deep, choking breaths.

All of a sudden, Nero was standing over us. "Pandora, Poison Ivy, get moving."

I glared up at him. "Ivy is done. Can't you see that? Give her a few minutes."

"There are no timeouts in life," he replied coolly. "When you're in the middle of a battle, you cannot take a few minutes."

"We're in a gym, not on a battlefield," I argued, standing to face him. "Even soldiers get to rest sometimes."

"You can rest when you're dead."

I frowned at him. "Stop being such a hard ass."

Ivy had been through a lot today. She hadn't fared well against the dog—nor her opponent afterward. She'd faced Mina, one of the Legion brats. The hand Mina had cut off of Ivy was still twitching, even though Harker had healed it back onto her.

Harker was standing over us now too. Damn, these guys moved fast. "Nero, I like her," he said with a chuckle.

Nero glowered at him, but he saved his lecture just for me. "I warned you that your mouth would get you into trouble. If you can't learn to keep it shut, you won't survive here."

I met his stare, too stubborn to look away. I knew that I should behave, that I should be frightened. The angel's power was mind-shattering. But I was too angry to be rational or even scared. I chalked it up to my protective streak, to my need to help my friend. I kept glaring at him.

"Careful," Nero warned.

"Or what?" I demanded.

"Can't you give the poor girl a rest, Nero?" said Harker.

"Very well." He waved Ivy away. "Go sit at the side, dead girl. Tomorrow when everyone else is eating lunch, you will be running." As Ivy wandered off, looking both relieved and anxious, he turned his stare on me again. "Now, Pandora, you will take her laps too."

"Come on, Nero. Give her a break," Harker protested.

"There are no breaks here," declared Colonel Hard Ass. "If she doesn't want her friend to run, she has to pick up the slack."

Harker opened his mouth to say something, but I was faster. "I'm fine. I'll take the laps," I told him. I looked at Nero, my chin lifted with stubbornness, and I set off running down the track once more.

Anger and the stubborn need to show Nero that I wouldn't back down carried me through most of the laps, but on the final one my mind could no longer ignore the signals my body was screaming at it. My legs buckled, and I stumbled to the ground.

"Serves her right for talking back to an angel," Mina chuckled to her running companion.

"This will teach her her place," he agreed as they zipped past me.

Another pair of Legion brats passed, piling on their own taunts. I struggled to pull myself up, but my body wasn't listening.

"If you're talking, you're not hurting enough," Nero's voice called out from across the gym. "Six more laps for the four of you."

Joy bubbled up inside of me, curling my lips into a smile.

"You too, Pandora," Nero said. "Six more laps. If you can smile, you can run."

He shouldn't have been able to see my smile. The man had the eyes of a hawk.

"Get up, or I'll add another six," he told me.

Damn him. I pushed against my own exhaustion, struggling to no effect.

Harker ran over to me. "Here," he said with a smile. "I thought you could use a hand."

"Thanks," I said, trying to return the smile.

But I was too tired to smile. I did manage to move my lips, but I don't think I pulled off anything more than a pained-looking expression. Harker reached down, locking his arm with mine to pull me to my feet. He'd sure been helping me a lot. Ok, he'd been helping everyone. But he'd been helping me even more. Probably because Nero had it out for me. That damn angel was a slave driver. This guy was the nice one. From what I could tell, they were best friends, which was surely one of Earth's greatest mysteries. How could two such very different people be friends?

"Get running, Pandora," Nero commanded.

"He means well," Harker told me. "He just wants to push everyone so they will be strong enough to survive the initiation ceremony."

"I think he has it out for me."

"He does seem harder on you," he agreed. "He's not usually this hard on anyone. You must be special."

I rolled my eyes. "Lucky me."

He chuckled. "You're going to be ok," he told me.

"Of course I am. I'm too stubborn to die," I replied, finally managing a smile. Then I set off running again.

A loud horn sounded in the hall as I finished my last lap. My hopes for a release from this torture were dashed when Nero began dividing us up into pairs for combat training. At least that's what he called it. My sparring buddy Jace, the biggest and meanest of the Legion brats, quickly turned it into beat-the-crap-out-of-Leda training. By the end of our so-called fight, I had a black eye, a fat lip, and the side of my body felt like it was on fire. But at least we weren't using swords right now.

"You weren't in many fights before you came here, were you?" Harker asked me as he healed my wounds with magic.

"I've been in lots of fights," I told him. "But I'm smart enough to fight from a distance when my opponent is much bigger and stronger than I am."

"Avoidance is not a strategy here," Nero said, stepping up to us. "You won't always be able to run away. You need to learn to handle yourself in every situation." He tossed me a wooden staff. "Attack me."

I glanced over at Harker, who seemed to be amused about something. I wasn't sure if he was laughing at Nero or at me. I wouldn't have blamed him if he was laughing at me. I was a joke. I couldn't fight at all. Nero was right about that. Damn angel. I hated it when he was right.

I moved cautiously toward Nero, then swung my staff. He parried my strike, then whacked me on the back with his staff.

"Too slow, Pandora," he chided me. "You're holding back. Stop standing there like a scared little girl and attack me like you mean it."

I charged forward, straight at him. Surprise flashed in his eyes for a moment, like he'd never expected me to do anything like that. Well, I was full of surprises. His surprise cost him a valuable split of a second, allowing me to land a solid strike to his ribs. I swung my staff around for a second blow, but my luck had run out. Nero caught my staff mid-strike, tearing it out of my hands. As my weapon abandoned me, I threw myself against my opponent, tackling him to the ground.

At least that was the plan. He rolled as he hit the ground, taking me with him. His hands tightened around my arms, and he slammed me to the floor. My back hit the rubbery ground with the resounding thump of defeat. I kicked, trying to get free, but he dug his knees into my legs, pinning them down. His hands were locked around my wrists, holding them to the ground above my head.

"Still too slow, Pandora," he said softly. A rare chuckle

buzzed on his lips, but it was gone so fast that I wondered if I'd only imagined it.

He was gone too, standing above me, holding his hand out to me. I took it, and when our skin touched, I felt that same spark of magic again. I disconnected myself quickly. This was starting to get too weird. What kind of magic was he trying to cast on me?

Everyone had stopped sparring to watch Nero kick my ass. The Legion brats were laughing their heads off, but I ignored them. Ivy met my eyes, a smirk slowly twisting her lips. Great. Now I was going to hear all night about how 'Colonel Sexy Angel' had pinned me to the ground. My roommates wanted to sleep with the angel almost as much as they wanted to kill him. Except Drake; he just wanted to be him.

Nero turned to face the other initiates, and they scrambled to continue sparring with their partner before he assigned anyone more laps around that gods forsaken track. Jace, my friendly partner, rubbed his hands together and grinned at me like he was going to enjoy making me bleed. I made a concerted effort not to wince. That would just rile him up even more. Instead, I stood there, waiting for him to come to me.

He surged forward, swinging his staff at my head. I ducked and darted away toward a curtain of thick ropes hanging from the ceiling. He was strong, but I was quick. I retreated toward the wall, and he followed, glee singing in his eyes. When he swung at me again, I hopped onto the climbing wall, running up it. He followed, trying to grab me, but I snapped my leg out in a sharp kick. My shoe slammed into his face, and he fell to the ground. I grabbed one of the ropes dangling from the ceiling and jumped down. As he blinked repeatedly, trying to focus his eyes, I knotted the end of the rope around his ankle. I looped the other end of the rope around one of the bars on the wall and heaved. Up on the ceiling, the rope slid across the pulley, yanking Jace off his feet. I tied the end of the rope on another of the lower wall bars, then passed under my opponent. He was hanging upside down fifteen feet up, kicking and swinging his arms around as he rained down curses upon me.

I just laughed. And I wasn't the only one. Most of the other initiates were laughing too—all were, in fact, except for the Legion brats.

"Come with me."

I jumped at the sound of Nero's voice right behind me. He really needed to stop sneaking up on me like that.

"You're in trouble," the Legion brats chanted as I followed Nero out of the gym. They had the maturity of four-year-olds.

Once we were alone in the hallway, Nero closed the door behind us and turned his marble stare on me. "What do you think you're doing?"

"Fighting."

"You were supposed to defeat your opponent using your staff, not gymnastics ropes."

I shrugged. "Some people would call that resourceful."

"This is not how we do things here."

"Well, maybe it's about time someone changed that."

Nero shook his head slowly. "I knew you were trouble. This is not Ultimate Street Fighter 2020, Pandora."

"You could have fooled me. What the hell was up with that blast door? Or the dog? That's street fighting at its dirtiest."

He watched me, his eyes cold. "This is the Legion of Angels," he continued, as though I hadn't said anything of consequence. "In the Legion of Angels, we use proper weapons in combat, not ropes and debris off the street. When we pick this up again tomorrow, you will use your assigned weapon—and *only* your assigned weapon—to fight your opponent. And you will continue to do that until you master the art of civilized combat."

That was rich coming from him. Nothing about this training was civilized. But I couldn't say that, so I made a joke instead.

"My assigned weapon? And here I was hoping for one of those cool flaming swords," I teased.

"The fire sword is an angel's weapon. A dignified weapon. It is difficult to wield."

"Well, I have to learn to use it sometime. Or should I wait to learn it until I'm an angel so I can inadvertently burn off my own wings. That's just not *dignified*."

His brows lifted. "What makes you think you will ever become an angel?"

"I figured it couldn't be that hard." I smiled pleasantly at him. "You did it."

"Careful," he warned, his voice low and dark.

"I always am."

That elicited a snort. "You may enjoy playing with fire, Leda Pierce, but I'm not letting you anywhere near a fire sword until you learn to tame your wild fighting. And that wild mouth of yours."

"Maybe I can't be tamed," I countered. I just couldn't help myself. There was something seriously wrong with me.

"I've broken wilder souls than yours," he said, his words a fierce promise he obviously had every intention to keep.

I had a sinking suspicion that 'breaking' involved thousands of laps around the track and pushups. Lots and lots of pushups. And maybe putting me in a room full of those hellish dogs.

"Now get moving, initiate." He motioned toward the door. "Back to the gym."

The Legion brats smirked at me as we rejoined the others in the gym. They were clearly happy about the telling-off I'd received. Jace was back on the ground and tapping his staff against his hand, his eyes tracking my progress across the room. Yeah, he was just waiting to jump me in the halls when no one was looking. I'd have to start carrying around that special blend of pepper spray Bella had mixed up for me. It might not have been a Legion-approved weapon, but I definitely approved of anything that would prevent me from being beaten to a bloody pulp.

"Your first month is over," Harker declared to the crowd as Nero joined him. "Congratulations on not dying."

Some of the initiates laughed.

"Tonight, the Legion is hosting a party at Club Firefall," he continued. "It starts in one hour. And you are all invited."

Someone dared to expel a celebratory cry.

"There will be members of the Legion of Angels present," Nero said. "Show respect. Don't mouth off. They are not as forgiving as I."

A few people laughed. Nero was as forgiving as a cactus. And those cold, unforgiving eyes were trained on me, as though he thought I was going to stroll up to the Legion soldiers in Firefall and start egging them on. I winked at him, which only made his eyes smolder more. As my staring contest with Colonel Hard Ass continued, I slowly began to realize the other initiates were filtering out of the gym.

"Come on, girl," Ivy said, wrapping her arm around me. "Let's get cleaned up, grab some food, and then party!"

I glanced at her. The promise of a party had really brightened her mood. When I looked back at Nero, the angel was gone, as though he'd disappeared into thin air.

CHAPTER TEN
Firefall

DEMETER, THE LEGION canteen, was packed. Like everything at the Legion, where we ate was organized into a strict hierarchical structure. We initiates sat at the two loud tables beside the tray drop-off point. Past our tables sat the sea of soldiers who'd actually made it into the Legion, ordered by rank all the way to the single head table at the other end of the room. That's where Nero, Harker, and anyone else level six or above sat. There were only eight of them currently here in New York, and Nero was the only angel of the group. The gods didn't grant wings to just anyone. I tried not to dwell on the impossibility of the task ahead of me. A task was only impossible if you'd decided it was.

Ivy and I grabbed our trays and headed for the food counters, but Jace and his band of brats barred our way.

"Hey, ladies," he drawled. "You look awfully tired. How about we help you carry your trays?"

I glanced up at the mirrored ceiling to make sure no one had scribbled 'idiot' on my forehead. Nope. Not this time. A few of the Legion brats had done it last week after one of them knocked me out during combat training.

"We're fine," I told them, holding onto my tray.

I'd use it to defend myself if I had to, no matter how much Nero might lecture me about 'inappropriate weapons' later. Even now, I could feel the angel's stare burning across the expanse, boring into me.

"You don't look fine," Mina said. She was a close second to Jace in terms of outright obnoxiousness. Her gaze flickered to Ivy. "We saw this poor girl collapse on the track. Maybe it was that beating I gave her before. How's your hand?"

The other brats snorted.

I stood up tall, staring them down. "Back off."

"You weren't holding up so well yourself, were you, Pandora?" Jace taunted. When Nero called me Pandora it was at least ten percent charming. When this asshole did it, it was one hundred percent aggravating. "Tripping over your own feet." He chuckled. "Now that must have been embarrassing."

It really had been, especially with Nero standing there, telling me to get up. I'd wanted to prove to him that I was as tough as the rest of them, but all I'd succeeded in was demonstrating how out of my league I really was.

I'd always considered myself fit and a better runner than most. But Nero's idea of a good runner varied enormously from my own. He expected people to run a mile in under three minutes. He wasn't interested in how impossible that was because supernaturals lived by different rules, he said. He'd once responded to my comment by running a mile in two minutes without breaking a sweat. It had taken enormous restraint not to give into the urge to remind the angel that he was running with all his gods-granted pistons firing, whereas our bodies were still mostly human. He would have just called it an excuse.

"You didn't look so great yourself dangling from your ankle," I shot back at Jace. "Did all your wild flailing make you finally fall out of the rope, or did they have to pull you back down like a hooked fish?"

Jace leaned forward. "Didn't they teach to respect your betters out there on the butt-end of civilization?" Each word pulsed with pure malice.

"No, they just taught us to stand up to people who thought they were," I said, grabbing Ivy's hand and pushing past the brats.

"I'm looking forward to meeting you in the ring again, Pandora," Jace called out after me.

I just kept moving. They didn't try to stop us, probably only because Nero and Harker were still watching. Standing up to those bullies was probably going to come bite me in the ass later, but I was too mad to care about that right now.

"They are so full of themselves," Ivy said to me as we loaded up our plates.

"Don't worry about them," I told her. "They're Wonder Bread. All fluffy and pretty on the outside, no substance on the inside."

"Yeah. Just because they've been groomed from birth to join the Legion, that doesn't mean they're better than we are." Ivy laughed glumly.

"They aren't."

"Really. I'm all for optimism. Hell, it's all that's gotten me through these past few weeks. But every one of those six has one angel parent. Most of them have another parent in the Legion too. How are we supposed to compete with them?"

"This isn't a competition against others," I told her. "Only against yourself."

VAMPIRE'S KISS

"Tell that to them when we face them in the fighting ring," she grumbled. "If they weaken us, we won't make it. And people like that don't want anyone else to make it. They think we aren't good enough for the Legion. They've been Legion families for generations. They always make it high in the ranks. Some of the magic the gods grant people passes through to their children. It's easier for them to unlock magical abilities than for nobodies like us."

I wrapped my arm around her and said, "Don't even think about them. We're a team, and we *will* make it through this. They might be bursting with magic, but we have dogged determination and our will to survive on our side. Stubbornness trumps raw power every time."

Ivy snorted.

"Now, come on. Drake is waving us over."

We joined him at the table and began devouring our dinner. I'd expended several thousand calories today, and I had only half an hour to replenish them.

"What's wrong?" Drake asked Ivy, who was mostly just staring down at her food.

She didn't say anything.

"The brats tried to get under our skin. But we're not letting them," I reminded Ivy.

"Screw the brats and their pretty plastic parts." Drake put his arm around Ivy, hugging her to him.

That's when I saw it in her eyes. She liked him. In a romantic way. As I sucked on my chocolate shake, I wondered if Drake realized it too.

◈ ◇ ◈ ◇ ◈

After dinner, we hurried back to our room for a quick shower. Then, for the first time in a month, we changed into something that hadn't come out of the Legion's closets. I slipped into my favorite pair of jeans and a lace-trimmed tank top Tessa had put into the suitcase Calli and the girls had sent over last week. And, just because I was feeling adventurous, I put on a pair of high-heeled boots.

Ivy had selected a pair of red leather pants and a see-through black mesh top with strategically-placed arrangements of lace. The heels on her scrappy gold sandals could have staked a vampire. Drake was sporting a pair of dark jeans and a muscle t-shirt that read 'I may look like an angel, but I dance like a demon'. Ivy had bought it for him before they'd joined the Legion. Maybe I should get one for myself, if only to see the appalled expression on Nero's face when I wore it in front of him. I snorted at the thought.

A kaleidoscope of flashing lights beamed down on us at Club Firefall. Our fellow initiates were all letting their hair down tonight, relishing in their freedom for the first time in a month. To the heavy, infectious beat of music, we danced and drank and let loose in a way none of us had in over four weeks—or, in my case, forever. There was something about a month of putting your body through one punishment after the other that made you appreciate life in a whole new way. For this one night, I was free.

As the song ended, I stepped off the dance floor with my five roommates, making a beeline for the cornucopia symbol hanging over the bar. Two Legion brats cut us off.

"Hey, Drake. And ladies." One of the guys laughed.

His buddy was equally jolly, and it wasn't just from the rum I smelled on his breath. "So, we were wondering." More snickering. "Are you even a real man?"

"What are you talking about?" Drake said.

"You're staying in a room of girls."

"Exactly." A smile spread across his lips. "I'm staying in

a room with five women. Take a moment to think about that."

Then Drake returned to the dance floor with our three female roommates, who danced all around him. The two brats watched him with obvious annoyance, then left in a huff.

"They had that one coming," Ivy laughed, then hurried to join our roommates.

But I was thirsty. I continued on to the bar and ordered a water. I'd already had way too many of those bombastic cocktails, and I wasn't even sure what was in them. Something that made me really happy. Or maybe that was just my temporary freedom.

"Playing it safe?" Harker said, glancing down at my water as he sat down on the barstool beside me. He had a bombastic cocktail, blue edition.

"Well, I'm supposed to be behaving myself," I replied. "Showing respect. Not mouthing off."

"Basically everything you excel at."

I grinned, lifting my glass. "Exactly."

We clinked glasses, then fell into silence.

"How are you doing?" Harker asked me after a few moments.

"Great, now that I've eaten. It takes more than a few laps around the track to kill me."

"You're doing well. Don't give up."

"I wasn't planning on it," I replied, then lowered my voice. "Ok, what's their problem?"

He followed my gaze to the trio of Legion soldiers at the other end of the bar. They'd been staring at us since Harker had sat down beside me.

"Legion officers and initiates don't hang out," he said. "Often?"

"Ever." He smiled at me. "But I like you. It takes a lot of guts to talk back to Nero."

"He says I have no sense of self-preservation."

Harker threw back his head and laughed. It was a perfect, honest-to-goodness laugh, without pretense or ulterior motives. It felt nice to be talking to someone who wasn't trying to get something out of me.

"Of course you don't," he told me. "That's what makes you so much fun. No one has talked back to Nero in a long time. It's good for his ego, keeps it from getting too inflated."

"You're his friend," I reminded him. "You shouldn't want me to antagonize him."

"Nero and I have a complicated relationship. We're brothers in everything but blood."

"I have a complicated relationship with my family too," I said. "Half the time we want to kill one another, but I'd never let anyone hurt them."

"You are a noble soul, Leda Pierce." He dipped his chin to me, then stood, going over to join Nero, who'd just entered the bar.

I watched them for a few moments. Whatever they were talking about, it looked serious. Maybe they were debating fresh new ways to torture us initiates come tomorrow morning. As I continued to watch them, Ivy and Drake spun and pivoted off the dance floor to join me at the bar.

"This is *crazy*," Ivy said, plopping down beside me. She helped herself to my water. "They are both staring at you."

I looked back at Nero and Harker. She was right. Whatever the two of them were arguing about in hushed tones, it seemed to have something to do with me. I shook off the thought. Not everything was about me.

"Harker seems to like you." Ivy fluttered her eyelashes at me.

"I'm pretty sure he's only being nice to me to annoy Nero."

Ivy glimpsed past my shoulder. "They are both *still* staring at you, Leda." Ivy began to fan herself.

"Should I get you some more water?" I asked her drily.

Ivy laughed. "No, I'm good. Come on."

She grabbed my hand, leading me onto the dance floor. I could still sense Harker and Nero watching me as Ivy and I danced. I was almost disappointed when they turned and walked away, which was definitely not something I should be feeling about anyone—least of all those two.

Ivy waved her hands in front of my face. "Earth to Leda. Are you listening?"

"Sorry. I was just distracted. What did you want to say?"

Ivy chuckled. "You're in trouble, girl."

"What do you mean?"

"They like you."

"Who?"

"Harker and Nero."

"No," I denied immediately.

Ok, maybe *too* immediately. A slow smile twisted Ivy's lips.

"Harker was just helping me," I explained. "And Nero is determined to kill me, one hellish obstacle course at a time."

"No, they like you." A slow smile twisted her lips. "And I heard something about Nero."

I waited for her to elaborate, but when she didn't, I said, "What did you hear?"

"That he doesn't usually oversee initiate trainings. In

fact, he hasn't done it in years. But something made him do it this time."

"Lucky us."

Ivy chuckled, bright and devilish. "I have a feeling I know what made him do it. Or who." She wiggled her eyebrows at me.

"No."

"Do you want to bet?"

No. I wasn't crazy enough to bet on the intentions of an angel. And what if he *had* become our trainer because of me? What if this was his way of cracking my secret? A shiver rippled through my body.

"They both like you," Ivy said again.

Ok, maybe I could see Harker liking me. He'd admitted that Legion officers didn't socialize with initiates, and yet he'd talked to me in front of everyone. He'd also been nothing but really nice to me ever since I'd arrived at the Legion.

But Nero? No way. He'd made the last month of my life a living hell.

Before I could ponder this further, however, men decked out in black leather flooded into the club, surrounding us all.

CHAPTER ELEVEN
Vampire's Kiss

THE FIGHT BROKE out all around me. The men in black looked like mercenaries. I didn't see any markings on their clothing to indicate they belonged to a larger organization. And they were all human. That, at least, was in our favor.

What wasn't in our favor were the numbers. The mercenaries outnumbered us two-to-one, and they were armed with enough knives to make an assassin weep with envy.

One of the men ran at me. I evaded, dashing toward the bar. I dialed up the magic smoke machine used to make the bombastic cocktails to full power. Multi-colored smoke poured out of the Magitech machine, spreading everywhere in the club. It was damn near impossible to see, but it must have been worse for the mercenaries. If we could see the attackers even a little better than they could see us, that might be the advantage we needed. Plus, we could depend on our other senses.

Another mercenary emerged from the glowing smoke. Towering two heads above me and built to crack rocks with his biceps, he was a beast of a man. He swiped a knife at me. I dashed away. He was swinging that thing hard enough to take my arm off, and I was actually rather attached to the thing. He continued to slash and swipe, forcing me into a retreat. My back was against the bar.

His knife slammed down, piercing the wood countertop. I'd barely moved my hand away in time. This guy wasn't fooling around. Maybe Nero had been right after all. I couldn't always run away. My eyes flickered to the mercenary's knife in the counter. It was wedged pretty tightly in there. That didn't seem to bother him. He was already drawing another one.

I jumped up onto the counter and gripped the handle of the stuck knife, using it to pivot myself around. As I slid around that point, I kicked out, slamming my foot hard against the mercenary's head. He fell to the ground, knocked out cold.

Hardly believing my luck, I hopped off the counter to look for his friends. I found them all on the floor, most of them unconscious but a few dead. Three of my fellow initiates had been stabbed, but none of them were dead. It could have just as easily gone the other way for us. What the hell had happened here? Why had these men attacked us?

It was then that I saw what fear and adrenaline had prevented me from realizing earlier. We initiates hadn't been the only ones in the club tonight, but we were the only ones standing here now. The mercenaries had gone straight for us. The Legion soldiers hadn't lifted a finger to help us. In fact, they were nowhere in sight.

The colorful steam blew away, as if dismissed by magic, and I saw the Legion soldiers step into the club. Nero was at the front, followed by Harker and Captain Somerset—and then a few more Legion soldiers I didn't know, including the ones who'd been gawking at me and Harker.

"They set us up," I said to Ivy, but the glare in my eyes was solely for Nero. "This was another one of their tests."

"Yes, it was a test," Nero said, addressing the whole room. "Everything is a test. You knew this going into the Legion. Only the strong survive." He set a bottle and a goblet down on the bar counter. "You will drink once more from the Nectar of the Gods, a stronger dose this time. Those who are strong enough will make the transition and gain Vampire's Kiss, the first ability in the Legion. You will be one of us."

He didn't say what would happen to those who were not strong enough. That much was already obvious.

"Form a line," Nero commanded.

And like good little initiates, we did as he said. I was near the back of the line this time. I watched in horror as six of my fellow initiates died before it was finally my turn.

I took the full goblet from Nero, chugging down the crimson liquid as fast as I could, praying that I didn't throw it up again. I removed the possibility of my own death from my mind. It wasn't helping.

I neither died nor threw up. I didn't even shake or spasm. Not this time. This time when I drank from the Nectar of the Gods, I wanted more. The liquid danced across my tongue in a symphony of sensations I couldn't get enough of. I looked down into the empty goblet, bemoaning that I'd drunk it so fast. As Nero reached for the goblet, I latched onto his arm, holding onto it with sheer desperation.

"More," I said, my voice thick with need.

That elicited a response on that granite face. Surprise flashed in his eyes. I tried to grab the bottle that held the Nectar, but he reached out, catching my hand. A shock of static electricity sizzled across our hands.

He opened his mouth to speak to me, but then must have thought differently of it. His hand locking mine in an iron grip, he pulled me away from the bar. "Come on, initiates. Get moving." He motioned to Harker. "Take over."

Harker gave us a curious look, but he did as Nero had asked. He refilled the goblet and was handing it to the next initiate in line as Nero pulled me out of the room. The hallway we entered was dark and empty. Except for the two of us.

"What is it, angel?" I laughed. "Taking me aside to have your way with me?"

He looked at me, his face unreadable. "You're drunk."

"What of it?" I tried to pry his hand off of me, but Sir Ironfist refused to budge. So I traced my other hand lightly across his fingers. He had surprisingly soft skin for the gods' hand of justice.

He watched my hand, as though he weren't sure what to make of what I was doing. "You're drunk on the Nectar."

"And?"

"How do you feel?"

I cracked a smile. "Worried about me?" I dipped my lips to his fingers and kissed them.

His hand sprang open, releasing me. "This is serious, Leda."

I stepped in closer, draping my arms over his shoulders. "Not Pandora this time? Mmm, you must *really* like me."

A voice inside of my head was screaming at me to stop, demanding what the hell I was doing. I didn't listen to it. Instead, I leaned in even closer, pressing my chest against his. I brushed my nose across his neck and inhaled. His scent flooded me, that dizzying delectably masculine flavor of sex and angel.

"You smell nice."

"You should be sick or in pain, not wanting more," he said.

"But I do want more." I traced my finger across his lower lip, and he grew very still.

"You are not yourself." Magic burned behind his eyes, an emerald fire just waiting to be released.

"Maybe this is who I really am," I whispered against his ear.

My new fangs burned my gums, a primal need beyond mere hunger cascading through me. I dipped my mouth to his neck, and every beat of his pulse against my lips filled me with a fresh throb of excruciating desire. I had a fleeting thought that I *really* wasn't myself, but the mindless, yearning nymphomaniac who'd taken hold over me tossed that thought right back out—along with all sense and reason. It was only me, the beautiful angel in front of me, and the agonizingly large distance between us.

I reached out and brushed back the caramel lock that had fallen over his forehead. As soft as silk, it glowed in the golden shimmer of the overhead Magitech lights.

"You're so pretty. Like an angel." I giggled at my own joke. "I bet you taste as good as you look." My fangs caressed his neck in slow, wide circles. I could feel his blood throbbing to the surface of his skin, daring me to taste him.

I dared.

My fangs broke his skin, and his blood flooded into my mouth. But it didn't taste like blood. It tasted like pure ecstasy. Better than the Nectar. Better than anything I'd ever tasted in my life. It tingled my tastebuds and slid down my throat, at the same time relieving and stoking the wanton need raging inside of me, my desire growing every time I drew him into me. His blood burned through mine, igniting it, setting off a chain reaction of raw arousal that shook me so hard I could hardly stand. I had to have more.

Nero caught me as I swayed, his hands on my hips. I clawed desperately at him, pulling him closer as I drank down his spicy sweetness. He groaned, grabbing me roughly, throwing me against the wall. He drew my head up so my eyes met his. They weren't cold anymore. They were smoldering like a volcano.

"I need you," I moaned, arching my back.

His gaze dipped to my breasts, which were swelling against my shirt. In a flash, his hands were on my top, tugging it over my head. He tossed it to the floor. His hand traced my naked skin all the way up my ribcage, teasing the edge of my bra. I lowered my hands to his belt, fumbling with the buckle. His hands slid around my bottom—then just froze.

"Harker," he said.

I glanced over my shoulder and saw Harker standing in front of the door, his face cautiously neutral. Sanity reared its ugly head, dragging me kicking and screaming out of the bottomless bit of desire that had overridden my rational brain. As my head began to clear, the world slowly shifted back into focus. I stepped away from Nero, scooping my discarded shirt off the floor.

"You're needed inside," Harker told Nero. His eyes flickered to me.

My cheeks burning, I tugged my top back on over my head. Nero touched his hand to his throat, healing the savage mess I'd made of it. Then he stepped past Harker to reenter the club. Harker looked at me for a moment, his expression uncharacteristically withdrawn, then he followed him.

I went next, my high crashing big time. I couldn't believe what I'd done. I had *bitten* an angel. I'd drunk from him. And I would have had sex right then and there with him in that hallway if Harker hadn't interrupted us. What the hell was wrong with me?

I looked across the room of eighteen remaining initiates. No one had died while I'd been making out with Nero, but someone could have. The thought sobered me up further.

"Welcome to the Legion of Angels," Nero addressed us.

As his eyes swept the crowd, I looked away. I couldn't look at him. Not now. Not after what had passed—and almost passed—between us.

"You have been given the gods' first gift," Nero continued. "But you haven't survived yet. You will need to control the hunger that comes with the gift." He glanced at me. "You will need to learn to wield the strength, stamina, and speed. And learn to heal yourself by drawing on the lifeblood of others. Those are the powers of the Vampire's Kiss."

I brushed my finger across my lips. I could still taste him.

"Everything you've done so far has led up to this point," said Nero. "Everything you do from now on out will determine your future at the Legion. And it begins now with your first mission."

A few people groaned quietly, but no one said anything.

"We will break you up into three teams. Major Locke will distribute your assignments now. If you get a one, you're with me. Two you're with him. And three you go with Captain Somerset."

Harker went around the room with a bowl of folded slips of paper, and the initiates took turns reaching in.

When it was my turn, I got a one.

"It looks like you're with me, Pandora," Nero said right behind me.

I turned around and gave him a wary look. His face had returned to that expressionless marble mask befitting of an angel. He'd given me a very different look back in that hallway.

Stop! I chided myself. There was no reason to think about that. No good would come of remembering that moment of temporary insanity.

Captain Somerset led her group out of the club first. Harker and his new soldiers went next. The rest of us followed Nero to the train station.

"Where are we going?" one of my teammates asked. He still looked ill from the Nectar. If only I'd had such an innocuous reaction to it.

"You'll find out when we get there," Nero said, motioning us onto the sleek, silver train.

CHAPTER TWELVE
Back to Purgatory

THE HIGHLIGHT OF the mission was when Lucy, one of my teammates, puked right next to my shoes during the train ride. Everything just went downhill from there.

Our voyage by train took only an hour, and I was surprised when we pulled into the station at Purgatory. My home town hadn't changed in the month since I'd seen it last. And yet… Everything seemed different. Fuller. It was as though a blanket had been torn from my senses, allowing them to truly breathe for the first time. My new eyes penetrated the shadows of the poorly-lit street. Every face was crisp, every street sign sharply in-focus. I could hear so much more—every step, every whisper, every breath. I could have done without my newly heightened sense of smell. I'd never realized before how much Purgatory smelled of garbage.

We all walked in silence behind Nero. He didn't explain why we were here of all places, in my home town. And I didn't ask. Neither of us even mentioned that it was my home town. It didn't matter anyway. Whatever we were doing here, it didn't have anything to do with me.

As he moved through the town, everyone stopped and

stared. We'd changed into our new uniforms during the train ride. We certainly were an impressive sight to behold, seven soldiers of the Legion of Angels, decked out in leather blacker than the night itself. And the citizens of Purgatory were clearly impressed. After all, it wasn't every day that the Legion came to town.

Nero led us to the Legion's local office. Unlike the impressive skyscraper that housed the New York branch, this one was just a room attached to the Pilgrims' temple of worship. The Pilgrims greeted us as we arrived. I recognized a few of them from all the times they'd cornered me on the streets to spread the gods' message. They didn't seem to recognize me, however; they didn't see past the Legion uniform. To the Pilgrims, the Legion's soldiers were the next closest thing to gods. *Especially* the angels. The raw adoration in their eyes when they looked at Nero made me downright uncomfortable, but he didn't seem to care. With professional efficiency, he ushered us all into the Legion office, then closed the door, leaving the Pilgrims alone in the hallway to finish another round of bowing and praising his unerring holiness.

A smile tickled my lips as I wickedly wondered what the Pilgrims would have thought about Nero's recent lapse in 'unerring holiness' with me back at Firefall. He wasn't a saint. He wasn't a machine. He was a man.

The realization intrigued me almost as much as it scared me out of my wits. Nero was powerful, dangerous, and though he'd demonstrated that he did sometimes succumb to the darker side of the human psyche, I wasn't sure there was room enough for any other feelings in him. Compassion just wasn't his color.

So I pushed all thoughts of his humanity out of my mind, returning my attention to the matter at hand—and the very small and sterile room we were standing in. A jail cell covered one wall of the room. A desk with a single chair sat in the other. And we stood awkwardly in the middle, trying not to bump or step on each other's toes as we waited for Nero to tell us why we were here.

He didn't keep us waiting long. "A group of unregistered vampires recently passed through this town."

'Unregistered' meant they'd been made outside of the system, just like that vampire I'd caught here a couple of weeks ago.

"Over the past two days, Legion soldiers have discovered dozens of dead bodies in New York," Nero continued. "We've linked those deaths to this group of vampires. They've fled into the Frontier, past the wall. We are going after them. The preference is on capturing them alive, so we can interrogate them. Kill only if necessary."

"How are we supposed to fight vampires?" Lyle asked. "They are so fast and strong."

"So are we. Fast, strong…" said Jace. "Brave." He smirked. "At least some of us are."

The Nectar of the Gods might have been a great indicator of someone's magic potential, but it was a shitty judge of character. Any one of the six initiates who'd died tonight was nicer than this jerk.

"You are just as fast and strong as a vampire now," Nero said. "You have the power. Now it's only a matter of waiting and seeing if you can tap into it."

Hence this little mission, no doubt. Piece by piece, the Legion was weeding us out until only the strongest were left. It was abhorrent. And yet here I was, playing right along with it. Desperation could drive people to do insane things.

"How many vampires are there?" Lucy asked quietly.

She was still looking queasy.

"We estimate ten."

"Ten," Toren echoed, shaking his head.

Nero opened the door. "Let's get moving."

We followed him down into the underground garage, where our ride awaited. Big, tough, and ugly, the off-road vehicle comfortably seated nine. As we piled in, I resisted the urge to point out that seven Legion soldiers plus ten vampires equalled eight more seats than we had. For all I knew, Nero was planning on tying our prisoners to the roof.

Jace and Mina sat in the back row, and they wouldn't let anyone else join them. Apparently, that row was just for the cool kids. Lyle, Lucy, and Toren squeezed into the middle row, which left me staring at the seat between the two brats. Jace tapped the back of the seat rest, his eyes daring me to sit back there. Yeah, this was going to be fun.

Nero stuck his head out of the window and called out, "Up here, Pandora. I want to keep my eye on you."

Jace and Mina burst into gleeful chuckles as though the world's biggest present had just landed in their laps. I slid the door shut and went to sit in timeout beside the teacher. There was a solid wall between us and the two other rows of seats, which at least meant the others couldn't hear Nero tell me off.

"I haven't done anything," I told him under the growl of the starting engine.

"Yet," he said. "But you have a talent for trouble. I need you focusing on this mission, not tying up two of your teammates with that spindle of cabling sitting in the trunk."

"I was doing no such thing."

"Not yet. But you *were* thinking about it."

"They are insufferable spoiled brats," I muttered. "And just because they have an angel for a parent, they think they can bully everyone else. That's just not right."

"And *you* have to fix it?"

"Yes." I folded my arms across my chest and tried to burn a hole through the windscreen with my non-existent laser beam magic. "Some things are just begging to be fixed."

"And some things will sort themselves out on their own," he said as the gate opened before us.

Beyond the borders of the wall, the Black Plains waited. The final battle of the war had raged here over two hundred years ago, but the lands were still scorched, a black mark that refused to fade. Maybe it would never fade, even if we managed to drive the monsters from the Earth.

Overhead a storm was brewing, swirling up the yellow-green clouds. The air was heavy and stank of monsters. I didn't see them anywhere, but I knew they couldn't be far away. They were never far away. There was a static charge in the air, a spark just waiting to go off. I hoped we wouldn't be here when it did.

"When I joined the Legion, we too had our fair share of insufferable angel spawn," Nero said, unbothered by the coming storm. I didn't think he was afraid of anything.

"What did you do about them?" I asked him.

"I *was* one of them."

I turned to look at him. "You?" I checked my surprise. "Wait, no. What am I saying? Of course you're one of them. You spent the last month making my life a living hell."

"That's my job."

But I wasn't done. "And you're all too pretty. Too perfect."

His lips twisted into a slight smile. "You seemed to appreciate that earlier tonight."

"I…" My cheeks flamed. "I don't know what came over me. The Nectar scrambled up my brain. I shouldn't have… Can we just forget that whole embarrassing incident happened?"

"As you wish."

If only I could forget. But the memory of his blood and magic coursing through my body like a burning river, priming every nerve, caressing every curve and peak—it overwhelmed me. I threw up my hands to cover my descending fangs.

"Sorry," I said through my hands.

"You need to learn to control that."

"I know. I'd always criticized vampires for being so weak-willed, so out of control. Controlling this—whatever it is—is even harder than I'd ever imagined."

"Unlike the vampires, we consume the magic straight from the source, so the urges hit us even deeper. That's why I have to be so hard on all of you. Without willpower, you had no chance of surviving Vampire's Kiss."

"You needn't worry about me. I have stubbornness to spare."

He chuckled, low and sensual. Wait, no, not sensual. That was just the Nectar talking again. There was absolutely nothing sensual about the angel sitting beside me. No reason whatsoever to reach across and touch… I yanked my hand back before I did something else I'd regret.

"The magic hit you harder than anyone," he observed. "That happens sometimes, that someone has a low magic tolerance."

"What can I do about it?" I asked hopefully.

"Nothing," he told me, dashing those hopes. "It's just a

part of you."

I slouched. "A weakness."

"Some would say so. My fellow brats used to taunt me about it relentlessly."

"You?" I gasped. "But you're like the biggest, strongest badass around."

"And yet I too am a magic lightweight. A single sip of Nectar is all it takes to get me drunk."

"A cheap date?" I teased.

He snorted. "You'll find, Leda, that we all have weaknesses, every single one of us, no matter how big or strong or badass we might be. You can't let them drag you down—and you can't let others drag you down because of them."

"Wow, that was a surprisingly good pep talk."

"Don't get used to it."

"I won't," I promised. "I know that tomorrow you'll be back to torturing me."

"I fear you've overestimated my magnanimousness. Your torture continues tonight."

"Thank you."

"You're welcome."

I chuckled, then sighed. "I do wish I didn't have so many weaknesses."

His brows arched. "Oh?"

"Yes, I have—" I stopped, narrowing my eyes at him. "If I tell you my weaknesses, you won't use that knowledge against me to more effectively torture me, will you?"

"I am well aware of your weaknesses, and I have already made use of that knowledge."

"Oh, really?" I sat on my hands. "Please enlighten me."

"You have a hard time bending to authority and holding your tongue, even in the face of danger. Which makes me wonder why you signed up to join the Legion in the first place."

I smiled at him. "I heard it's where all the hot guys hang out."

"See, *that* is exactly what I mean. No sense of self-preservation."

"I happen to have an excellent sense of self-preservation. I don't mouth off to people I can't take in a fight."

"And you think you can take me?" he asked doubtfully.

"I have a taser at my thigh and a bottle of pepper spray in my pocket." I smirked at him. "And you are too busy driving at the moment to put up much of a fight."

He met my eyes for a moment, then returned his attention to the road. "As I was saying, no sense of self-preservation. I could take you with both hands tied behind my back."

"Prove it."

He remained perfectly still—so still that I didn't think he was going to do anything. I kept my eyes on him the whole time anyway so I'd be ready if he did try anything. Well, he did try something, and I wasn't ready. He moved so fast that even my newly heightened senses couldn't keep up. One moment both of his hands were on the steering wheel and the next my wrist was handcuffed to the armrest. I yanked against my bindings, and a surge of electrical magic tore through my body.

"This isn't fair."

"Life never is," he replied. "But the scales do have a way of balancing out in the end. Which brings us to something else you need to work on."

"Revenge?" I growled at him through clenched teeth. I pulled on the handcuffs again, biting back a yowl when that didn't work out any better than last time.

"No." He tossed me the keys to the cuffs. "Learning to fight opponents bigger and stronger than you. Fighting from a distance isn't always an option."

Yeah, I couldn't slam his head into the steering wheel from a distance, for instance. Then again, I couldn't do it up close either. My hands now free, I tossed him the keys and the cuffs. He snatched them out of the air, and then they were just gone. I really had to figure out how he was doing that.

"Your performance at Firefall was an improvement over previous exercises," he said.

"Was that praise I heard?" I asked with a smile, rubbing my sore wrists.

"An observation. And I'd like to see more of that. No more fighting with inflamed dishtowels and broken mirror shards. I want to see you fighting with your body. And proper weapons."

"Like a sword? A sword has range."

"For instance."

"Geez, teacher, I'd love to, but you won't let me near a sword." I smirked at him.

"I said I wouldn't let you have a *fire* sword."

"Ah, but they're so pretty."

The hint of a smile hovered on his lips. "In truth, I am reconsidering letting you have a fire sword. Under proper supervision, of course," he added.

"Yours?"

"Yes. Harker would go too easy on you, and Basanti wouldn't go easy enough on you. You don't learn much if you spend the whole training session unconscious."

"I'll remind you of that the next time you shout 'loss of consciousness is no excuse for not running your laps, initiate!' at me."

"You are an initiate no longer. You are a soldier of the Legion of Angels."

"Then I guess you'll need to update your catchphrases."

"And you need to update your decorum," he told me. "I am your commanding officer."

"Does that mean I get to call you 'sir'?"

"It means you have to."

I snickered.

He shot me a hard look. "You are not taking this seriously."

"Did you expect anything different from me? Sir," I tacked on quickly, clearing my throat to swallow a second snicker.

"No."

"I'll behave myself now," I promised, folding my hands in my lap.

"That I seriously doubt, Pandora."

Nero parked the car just inside a grove of black-barked trees, then turned off the engine. Everyone piled out and followed him. We walked for about ten minutes, then he stopped at the crest of a hill.

"The vampires are just down the hill, hiding out in the ruins of those old buildings," he said, squatting down. He pointed down at the firelight flickering across the hill of trees below us, setting shadows into motion.

"There are a lot more than ten of them. It looks more like twenty," I observed.

"This changes nothing," he said coolly. "We will trap them as planned."

Then he instructed Jace, Mina, Toren, and Lyle to lay down a fire line around the camp. Enchanted with magic, flames would shoot up on it when activated. It was one fine piece of Magitech, and it must have cost a fortune.

As the others laid down the line, Nero, Lucy, and I stayed behind to watch the vampires' camp.

"These are loaded with vampire tranquilizers," Nero said, handing us each a gun. "It will knock them right out. But be careful. They will knock you out too."

"Much better than broken glass," I commented, patting the gun fondly.

"Broken glass?" Lucy asked me.

"That's how I took out my last vampire," I told her.

"With glass?"

"Well, technically I smashed his head into a mirror, then hit him over the head with a fire extinguisher."

Lucy's eyes grew wide. "You are kind of awesome, Leda."

I grinned at her. "Thanks."

The rest of our team had just returned, so we all headed down the hill. The vampires jumped to their feet when they saw us emerge from the woods, but most of them slumped back down again as soon as the reality of our Legion uniforms set in.

"I am Colonel Nero Windstriker of the Legion of Angels."

Gasps whispered across the crowd of vampires as they realized what his rank meant: our leader was an angel.

"You have been illegally turned," Nero continued. "Under the authority of the gods, I am placing you all under arrest. Surrender at once and no one has to get hurt."

The rest of the standing vampires sat down—all except for one. He must have been their leader. "We are outside the gods' rule now," he declared.

"There is nowhere on this Earth that is outside the gods' rule, not even out here on the Black Plains," said

Nero.

The vampire's lips drew up into a sneer. "We'll see."

His fearlessness put fire back into the hearts of the vampires—or maybe they'd just realized there were twenty of them against only seven of us. As they charged toward us, Nero set off the fire line. A wall of flames shot up all around the campsite, trapping the vampires inside. And us with them. I hoped Nero had thought this through. The six of us weren't veteran soldiers. We were newbies with one month of training under our belts. It had only been only a few hours since we'd gained the physical powers of vampires, and most of us weren't wielding those abilities at one hundred percent yet—or even at ten percent.

Thankfully, the blazing wall of fire around the campsite seemed to have distracted the vampires. We fired at them. Thanks to my new abilities—and my practiced preference for long-range attacks—I even managed to hit a few of them. As Nero had promised, the vampires went down instantly. This anti-vampire ammunition was awesome.

The vampires' numbers dwindled. A few of them were eyeing the fire wall, like they were thinking of escaping, but the flames burned too high. The ring of fire had effectively trapped the vampires.

Or so we'd thought.

The roar of a revving engine tore out of the ruins, followed by a vampire riding a motorcycle. It was the leader. He drove up a pile of debris, using it to jump onto what remained of the roof of one of the buildings. Broken shingles bounced off his wheels, raining down as he and his motorcycle leapt over the fire ring.

"Get these vampires chained and brought back to town. You're in charge, Pandora," Nero said, tossing me the controller for the flames as he ran after the motorcycle.

His shimmering wings spread from his back in a glorious tapestry of blue, green, and black—and then he flew into the air to give chase to the fleeing vampire. I stopped and stared at the beauty of his wings for a moment, but a charging vampire snapped me back into the fight. I shot him in the chest, then shot two more vampires. The fight was over.

When all the vampires were lying unconscious on the ground, I put out the flames. Then came the fun part. We tied up all of our prisoners and carried them back to our truck. We were much stronger than humans now, which was in our favor, but the vampires were heavier than humans too. And the hike was uphill the whole way. By the time we had them all loaded into the truck, it was an hour later, and we were sweaty, dirty, and tired.

And Nero still hadn't returned.

CHAPTER THIRTEEN
The Black Plains

IT TOOK US another two hours to drive back to town and stuff all of our vampire prisoners into the jail cell in the Legion's office room. Three hours had passed since Nero had flown off in pursuit of the escaped vampire, and he still hadn't returned.

"That doesn't bode well," I told the others.

"What do we do?" Lyle asked me.

The others all looked to me for guidance—even Jace and Mina. Apparently, the fact that Nero had put me in charge counted for something. I still couldn't fathom why he'd done that. Jace would have been the more obvious choice. He was stronger and better trained than I was, and in spite of his penchant for being a complete asshole, he did have the temperament to lead others. Even I, in all my pettiness, could admit that. But whatever Nero's reasons, he had put me in charge, and I was going to make full use of my authority.

About halfway along our journey back to town, I'd begun to have flashes of broken, bloody images. At first, they were just short bursts, disconnected and fleeting. But with every passing moment, the images grew more sustained and the sensations more painful. I was chained, beaten, and cut. Every lash of the whip drew a fresh pulse of pain, every slash of the knife etched agony into my quaking body. Someone was torturing me. And yet when I looked down, my clothes were intact and my skin unbroken.

They weren't torturing me, I realized. They were torturing Nero. When I'd drunk from him, when I'd taken his blood into me, something must have happened between us. We were linked. I'd heard about this in vampires, but I hadn't realized it happened to soldiers of the Legion as well. It appeared my temporary lapse in sanity was good for something after all. Maybe I could use this link to find Nero.

But how? I began to pace around the Legion office, trying to think things through. According to what I'd read, a blood bond between vampires was dependent on both place and time. In other words, the closer the linked pair of vampires were, the stronger it was. And the more time that lapsed since the blood exchange, the weaker the bond grew.

If our magic worked the same as the vampires' did, I could follow Nero's 'signal'. The closer I got, the more I should feel of what they—whoever *they* were—were doing to him. After the initial burst of sensations, my link to him had quieted down as we'd moved closer to the town. I wasn't keen on following the path of increasing pain, but this was no time for cold feet. Our connection was winding down by the minute. If I didn't leave now, I might lose his trail completely. I couldn't leave him to that torture.

With that decided, I turned to Jace. "Call the Legion. Tell them what happened." I looked at the vampires. One was stirring. I drew my gun and shot him full of more tranquilizers. "I'm going after Nero. You're in charge now."

This time when Jace looked at me there was no hatred in his eyes nor a sneer on his lips. He looked at me as though I'd lost my mind to want to go back out there, but he just nodded.

"It's dangerous on the Black Plains," Lucy piped in.

"It is," I agreed. "But I've tracked out there before." There had been a time when we were desperate for money and would take any job, even those on the Black Plains. "I know the area. I will find Nero. And I'll bring him back."

"We should come with you," Toren said.

I shook my head. "No. You need to stay here and watch the vampires. That is the mission. If they wake up, these bars might not hold them. There are a lot of people living in this town, and the local sheriff's department isn't equipped to handle nineteen wild vampires."

"*We* might not be able to handle them," said Lyle.

"I'll send you help," I promised, moving toward the door.

As I made my way toward the Legion motorcycle I'd spotted parked outside, I pulled out my phone and dialed Calli.

"Leda," she answered immediately. "Are you all right?"

"I'm here in town."

"I take it this isn't a social call."

"No," I told her, waving over one of the Pilgrims.

When he came to me, I pantomimed my need for the motorcycle's keys. He blinked once, as though he were starting to place my face, but he didn't let any memory of me stand in the way of him doing his job. He dropped the keys into my hand.

"The Legion sent us to apprehend some vampires who'd escaped onto the Black Plains," I told Calli. "Nineteen of them are sleeping in a jail cell in the local Legion office, guarded by five Legion soldiers with one month of training apiece."

"That sounds ominous."

"Do you think you could head over there to be their backup?" I asked her. "I know this isn't your job, but I'd really appreciate—"

"I'm heading over there now," she said.

"Thanks. I have to head back onto the Plains, but I'll see you soon." I hoped.

"Why are you going out there again?" she asked, a hint of reproach in her voice.

"I have to save our commander."

Reproach melted into curiosity. "Is that all he is?"

I didn't mention the blood drinking. Or anything else I'd done to Nero. It was just too embarrassing.

"I don't know, Calli," I said. "I have to go."

"Be careful, Leda. Angels are every bit as dangerous as monsters."

I hardly needed the warning. I *knew* how dangerous angels were. Or did I? Anyone in their right mind wouldn't even dream of talking back to an angel, let alone teasing one. I'd done both—multiple times. And I would continue on doing both as soon as he was back. Gods, Nero was right. I really didn't have any sense of self-preservation.

Well, I'd need that lack of fear out on the Plains, I decided as I hopped on the motorcycle and drove it toward the wall that separated civilization from chaos.

◆ ◇ ◆ ◇ ◆

I followed my link to Nero for about an hour, gritting my teeth against the steadily increasing waves of agony besieging my body, igniting pain receptors I hadn't even known I'd had. By the time I stopped outside an old castle beside a raging waterfall, the pain had reached tsunami levels.

On the plus side, I hadn't met any monsters on my way here. And I was freakishly stubborn. That was helping me bear the pain.

I snuck past a pair of vampires guarding one of the entrances. They were too busy shooting at mice to notice me. They must not have believed anyone but a complete crazy person would be all the way out here, trying to infiltrate their decaying castle. And, you know, they were probably right.

I stepped quickly and quietly down the halls, ducking and darting, running and hiding. I was trying to block out Nero's agony even as I struggled to follow it to him. It didn't help that there were vampires everywhere. What the hell was going on here?

I made it to the room where they were keeping Nero. Like all of the other rooms in this castle, half of the walls were falling apart. They'd stripped him down to only the leather pants of his Legion uniform and stapled him to one of the walls that was still standing. His torso and arms and feet were bare. Dozens of knives protruded from his chest and back, holding him to the wall. Blood dripped down his body in crimson streams, splattering the graveled ground at his feet. His head drooped, his eyes wild and unfocused behind a wet curtain of sweat-stained hair.

No one else was in the room. They must have been taking a break from torturing him. This was my chance, and I was going to take it. I would free Nero. And then I was going to hunt down the bastards who'd done this to him.

"Nero," I whispered as I came up to him.

He blinked down hard, trying to focus. "Leda?"

I touched his face. "I'm going to get you out of here."

He grunted as I began pulling the knives out of him. His head swayed.

"Hey, none of that," I told him, snapping my fingers in front of his eyes. "No passing out on me. You're too heavy for me to carry."

He coughed. "You're stronger now."

As I pulled the last of the knives from his body, he stumbled forward, nearly crushing me. "But I'm not strong enough to carry an angel." I leaned him against the wall. "I swear you must be made of gold bars or something."

And muscle, I added mentally as my eyes traced the contours of his body. Then, realizing what I was doing, I looked away.

He chuckled under his breath. "It's ok. I won't tell anyone."

"There's nothing to tell," I said quickly.

"There's much to tell. You can start with why you're here. You had orders."

"Screw orders. Someone had to save your ass. Sir," I tacked on with a smirk.

"This is insubordination."

"Punish me later. For now, I have to get you out of here." I looked around. "What's going on?"

A dark look fell over his face. "The rogue vampires are building an army. This operation is bigger than we'd thought. There are over a hundred vampires here. And, from the sounds of it, many more elsewhere."

"Why?"

"They are preparing for war."

"A vampire army, you say? Fantastic."

I pulled on his arm, inviting him to stand on his own.

He didn't budge.

"Get moving," I snapped.

His eyes rolled back.

"Get moving," I repeated. "You drill into us the need for willpower. Now show some willpower of your own."

"How can I argue with that?" he chuckled.

He pushed off the wall, but his arms quaked, collapsing. He coughed up blood. Shit. What had they done to him? No, never mind. I didn't want to know.

"You need to heal yourself," I told him.

"I don't have enough magic left for that."

"How did they drain an angel of his magic? You basically have an unlimited supply of it."

"Not unlimited. Only a lot," he said. "Even so, there are means to quickly drain an angel. They seem to know them."

I could hear people coming down the hall, probably Nero's torturers returning to finish the job. We didn't have much time.

I looked Nero in the eye and said, "Drink from me."

His gaze dipped to my throat, his lower lip quivering with hunger as he stared at me. He shook himself. "No."

"Stop being such a prude and just do it. You don't have the magic to heal yourself, so just take what you need from me." I zipped down my jacket, exposing more of my neck.

He caught my hand, stopping me, but his eyes had dipped once more to my pulsing neck. "That is not standard procedure."

"Look around, Nero. We're surrounded by a vampire army. This isn't a standard situation."

He met my eyes. "All right. But not the neck." He lifted my wrist to his mouth, his fangs descending.

"Is the wrist better?"

"It's more…detached," he said, then sank his fangs into me.

A sudden jolt of pain pierced me as he penetrated my skin—slowly replaced by a deep, aching throb. I leaned into him, gasping for breath even as the river of fire surging through me threatened to drag me under.

Nero's mouth lifted, looking at me. His stare penetrated me as surely as his fangs had. He brushed a finger across my lips, igniting a spark of magic between us.

Suddenly, he pulled away, putting some distance between us.

"Nero?"

He turned away from me. "Give me a moment."

I watched his back rise and fall as he drew in several deep breaths. His wounds sealed together before my eyes.

"Ok." He straightened and turned to leave. "Let's go." I caught a flash of magic pulsing in his eyes as he passed me.

We met a trio of vampires on our way out the door. They saw him—that he was free and unharmed—and fear flashed in their eyes. They stepped back. They didn't make it far. In a surge of fury, Nero charged at them, tearing them apart before they could even lift a hand against him. As the last one dropped dead to the floor, he turned and headed for the exit.

More vampire guards flooded inside, but Nero's rage knew no bounds. He strode down the hall, blasting them away with a hurricane of magic. It slammed into their bodies with the force of a high-speed train. Stone and plaster exploded all around us as bodies rained down from the ceiling. We ran all the way to the motorcycle.

"Don't think you can carry me and fly us back?" I teased him as he straddled the motorcycle.

"With that mouth, it's a wonder you're still alive."

I smirked at him. "You seemed to like my mouth just fine earlier."

He gave me a hard look. "Get on, Pandora." He grabbed my hand and pulled me onto the seat right beside him. "And try not to let go."

He sped off through the trees. The sound of the motorcycle's engine hummed over the rush of falling water, but it wasn't as loud as the engines roaring behind us. I glanced back to find three motorcycles hot on our tail.

"We've got company," I told Nero, turning to shoot one of them in the shoulder. "A werewolf. Hired help?"

"Just shoot them."

The tranquilizers were meant for vampires, but it took out that shifter just fine. His head dropped, and he fell off his motorcycle.

"How much damage can a werewolf take?" I asked Nero.

"The man turns into a five-hundred-pound wolf. I think he can survive a little tumble from his bike. Now stop worrying about the people trying to kill us and start shooting them."

I fired twice, knocking both vampires off their motorcycles too. "It's just that I don't really want to kill anyone."

"Then you're in the wrong line of work," he said sternly. His tone softened slightly as he glanced down at the gun holstered to my thigh. "You're a decent shot."

"Try not to sound so surprised."

"After all that's happened, I don't think you could possibly surprise me anymore."

"Oh, I'm sure I still can," I said with a smirk, holding onto him tightly as he accelerated across the Plains.

Everyone stopped and stared at us as our motorcycle roared into Purgatory. I'd like to think they were staring in awe of my spectacular rescue, but I was pretty sure they were just ogling the half-naked angel with me.

We'd only just parked the motorcycle when Harker exited the Legion office. He walked up to Nero and gave him a thorough once-over, his mouth quirking up in amusement at his friend's missing clothes.

"You lost something," he said.

"They lost more," Nero told him. "What are you doing here?"

"Babysitting nineteen vampires. Our girl here kept the team busy while she raced across the Black Plains to rescue you in a blaze of glory." Harker winked at me. "Your team called headquarters. Since my team was done with their mission, I brought them here to help you transport the vampires back to the city."

"Good," Nero said. "We need to get answers out of those vampires right away."

Harker set his hand on my shoulder. "You did the gods a service today by saving Nero. The Legion can't afford to lose any more angels."

"Any *more*?" I asked.

Nero shook his head at Harker.

"Thank you, anyway. You did a great job tonight," Harker said, grinning at me. "You might even get a medal."

"Not for disobeying orders, she won't."

Chuckling, Harker slapped him on the back. "I'm glad you made it, Nero. The Legion wouldn't be the same without your cheerful disposition," he declared as a truck with our two teams and the vampires passed by, presumably on the way to the train station.

"The vampires are building an army," Nero said. "This small group is just the tip of the iceberg."

"We need to go back to that castle," I told them.

"The Legion is sending a veteran team there," Harker said.

"This mission wasn't supposed to be so big. My team wasn't prepared to handle it."

"They did all right," Harker told him, looking at me.

I slowed my steps when I saw Calli standing outside of the Legion office, watching us. But I didn't stop. I was on a mission, and I wasn't supposed to stop until I was done. Even I knew that. So close and yet we might as well have been on opposite ends of the Earth. It sucked, but this was what I'd signed up for.

Nero's gaze slid from her to me. "Go."

"Really?" I asked, my expression brightening.

"Five minutes."

"Thank you," I said, touching his arm briefly before I turned and ran toward Calli.

"Going soft, Colonel," Harker said with a low chuckle as he and Nero walked off.

"Oh, shut up."

I kept running for Calli, sweeping her up into a hug. She laughed. I'd forgotten how much I loved that laugh.

"You're looking good, Leda. Strong," she added as I set her back down on the ground.

"For the longest time, I thought I might die, but I made it, Calli. I am stronger. I still can't fight with a 'proper' weapon according to the Legion, but I'm getting there, slowly but surely."

"You have always been strong. I know you can do this."

I smiled at her. "Thanks."

"I just wish you didn't have to."

Her eyes flickered to Nero. He and Harker had stopped beside the Legion truck outside the train station, and they were unloading the vampires.

"Be careful with that one," she warned me. "Angels always have an ulterior motive."

"I already know he's trying to kill me," I laughed.

"No jokes, Leda. This is serious. The Legion changes people. Power changes people. I've seen it happen."

"Back at the League of Bounty Hunters?"

"Among other places."

"I'll be careful," I promised. "Now I have to go. Talk to you later. Tell my sisters I love them."

Calli set her hands on my cheeks. "You're a good girl, Leda." She kissed me on the forehead, then turned and walked away.

I hurried down the street, arriving at the station as the last of the vampires was carried inside. I followed the prisoner procession to the train. Harker was standing outside. He grinned at me when he saw me.

"I meant what I said," he told me as we stepped onto the train together. "You were right to go after Nero."

"Nero doesn't think so."

He snorted. "Nero might be a stickler for the rules, but he's not without humanity. He didn't want to die at the vampires' hands."

"Is he human?" A month ago, I'd have been certain that he wasn't. Now, I wasn't sure anymore.

"Yes, even angels are still human under all the feathers and narcissism," said Harker.

I laughed.

"And he knows too much," he continued. "The vampires didn't break him, but if they'd had him a lot longer, they might just have been able to do it, no matter what Nero says."

Nodding, I took my seat beside Lucy. As the train took off, I wondered about that. The thought of Nero's humanity was more frightening than his inhumanity. Calli was right. I had to be careful with the angel.

CHAPTER FOURTEEN
Heaven

IT WAS ALMOST noon by the time we made it back to the Legion building in New York. We'd been awake all night, but rather than let us sleep, Nero ordered us all to the gym. Three hours later, I stumbled into my dormitory and fell onto my bed. I fell asleep the moment my head hit the pillow.

When I woke up, the sun was setting. I wiggled my toes and sat up. The dormitory was empty except for Ivy, who was sitting on her bed, munching enthusiastically on the cookies inside the tin wedged between her legs.

"Good morning, sunshine," she said with a smirk.

"Evening is more like it. Where is everyone?" I asked, stretching out my arms.

"Down at Demeter having dinner."

I walked over to her bed and sat down beside her. "And you?"

"I prefer something sweeter." She held out the tin. "Cookie?"

I dug in and pulled out a red velvet cookie. "Thanks." The first bite was a revelation, the second an addiction, and by the third I was wondering where this cookie had been all my life. "This is amazing. Where did you get those cookies?"

"My mom made them." Ivy wiped the tear from her eye, putting on a brave smile. "She is the best baker in all of New York. Maybe even in the whole world."

"She certainly gets my vote," I agreed, putting my arm around Ivy. "You *will* save her."

She blinked back more tears. "How do you know?"

"Because I have faith."

"I didn't take you for the gods-worshipping type." Her lip twitched.

"I'm not really. I don't sing hymns in the gods' temples and throw myself down on the ground in front of their shrines. But that's not the faith I was talking about. The faith I'm talking about is the belief that there is good in the world. The world is full of monsters, Ivy. We have to believe that there's hope for us, that everything will work out in the end. Otherwise, we're already lost."

"My mother would like you." Ivy smiled at me. "In fact, she already does."

"Oh?"

"I wrote to her about you. About how you've been helping me. She's happy I found such a good friend. Someday, I hope you can meet her."

"I'd like that," I said, squeezing her hand. "Let's make a pact: you and I. Whichever of us makes it to level seven first will heal your mother."

Her expression brightened. "Really? You'll help me?"

"I will always help you, Ivy. And if I make it to level seven first, I will heal her."

"Oh, you will make it. I'm sure you will. You're strong."

"Well, I am stubborn. I'm not sure about strong. I feel like I'm one of the weakest ones here."

"Not according to Colonel Sexy Angel. I heard him talking to Harker on the train ride back."

"What did they say?" I tried to keep my tone casual, even though I was burning to know.

"He told Harker to stop helping you so much because you're very strong, and you'll never reach your potential if he holds your hand the whole way."

I snorted. "Nero just wants to break me. It's his new personal goal."

"Or maybe he wants to hold your hand himself." She wiggled her eyebrows.

"I don't think he's much of a touchy-feely kind of guy."

"Leda, *everyone* is talking about what happened last night. How you blazed across the Black Plains to rescue Nero from a vampire army. Half of the Legion thinks you're really brave. The other half thinks you're out of your mind."

"And what do you think?" I asked her.

"That you're a little of both, of course." She paused, a slow smile twisting her lips. "Harker is saying you're a hero."

"Whatever that means."

She shrugged. "Apparently that you have the perfect balance of bravery and insanity."

I laughed. "At least someone is happy with me. I swear Nero is still thinking up a way to punish me."

"For saving him?"

"For disobeying orders."

"Well, he is an angel," she said, as though that explained everything. It probably did.

Or did it? After our discussions last night, I was beginning to realize Nero was more human than I'd thought. I wondered if he realized that too. Then again, maybe he was in denial. He probably saw humanity as a weakness.

A knock sounded on the door. Weird. In the whole month that we'd called this our room, no one had once knocked on our door. I was not counting the gigantic spitballs the brats had launched at it from across the hall. Honestly, I sometimes felt like I was living in a high school.

I walked to the door, my surprise only growing when I opened it to find Harker standing on the other side.

"I need to talk to you," he said to me. "Alone."

"I'll be right back," I told Ivy, then followed him into the hall, closing the door behind me.

He stood opposite me, his arms folded over his chest in a way that accentuated the muscles of both. But I wasn't here to admire his physique. He obviously had something to say to me. His mouth was hard, set, like he didn't know where to begin. I'd never seen him so nervous before—if I could even call it that. Harker hated to be the bad guy. He was probably just getting himself psyched up to say something I wouldn't like. Maybe he was here to deliver Nero's punishment.

"How's Nero doing?" I asked, inviting him to get on with it. Dragging it out would just hurt more.

"All right. Better than all right, in fact. That's what I'm here to talk to you about."

"Oh?"

"Nero is completely healed from his ordeal last night. It's nothing short of miraculous. From his report, his captors drained him of magic and blood. He was in a sad state when you found him. It should have taken him a week or at least an appointment with a good healer to be back to normal. And yet here he is in perfect health less than half a day later."

"He's an angel," I pointed out.

"After the vampires were through with him, he would have been too drained to heal himself."

I shrugged. "Magic works in mysterious ways."

Harker gave me a hard look. "He drank from you, didn't he?"

"What did he say?"

"I'm asking *you*."

But I was keeping my mouth shut. I had the feeling Nero wasn't supposed to have done that. Had he not protested that it wasn't standard procedure?

Harker sighed. "Nero won't admit to it either. It must be the first time he's ever lied to the Legion. Don't worry," he said quickly. "I won't tell."

"Is drinking from another Legion soldier against the rules?"

"Not exactly, but it is frowned upon. Especially a blood exchange between an angel and a first level soldier. The disconnect in power is too great. You drank from him too. Back before we left for the mission, after you'd sipped from the Nectar."

I didn't say anything. Maybe I was starting to learn the value of keeping my mouth shut.

"Nero is struggling with his inner darkness. I hope you know what you're doing, Leda."

Calli had said the same thing.

"Nero is your friend," I said.

"Yeah, he is. But he's also an angel. When you get your wings, you change. Like even more than you change when you first join the Legion."

"So you don't want to be an angel?" I asked him.

"Oh, I do. More than anything." A happy smile spread across his mouth. "And you?"

"I'm not sure I'm angel material."

"Oh, I think that you are. You're resilient."

"But I have trouble doing what I'm told."

He laughed. It was a beautiful sound, so encouraging, so full of good intentions. In the past couple weeks, I'd come to really appreciate Harker's laugh.

"Indeed you do," he said. "There's a party in Heaven tonight."

"I don't think I'm invited."

"Heaven, the Legion club," he clarified, laughing again. I could just listen to that laugh all night. "You should come and unwind. That's really important after a mission like the one last night."

"I'll think about it."

"I look forward to seeing you there." He took my hand, lifting it to his lips, then with a wink, he turned and walked down the hall.

As soon as I stepped back into my dormitory, Ivy practically pounced on me.

"And?" she asked excitedly. "What did Harker want?"

"He told me about a party at Heaven tonight."

"Harker asked you out?" She practically squealed.

"Uh, I don't think so. He just told me about the party."

But Ivy wouldn't hear of it. "Heaven is a VIP club for Legion members, level five and above only. I'd give my right arm to go there."

"Then you should come with me," I declared. "But no need to cut off your arm."

Ivy grinned at me. "Now let's pick out what you're going to wear on your date."

"It's not a date," I reminded her as she pushed me toward the closet.

"Honey, by the time I'm through with you, you'll have Harker eating out of your hand."

And on that foreboding note, she began pulling clothes out of the closet.

◆ ◇ ◆ ◇ ◆

When Ivy and I arrived at the club, the bouncer waved us right in. He didn't even need to check the list. Harker must have talked to him personally, something Ivy was quick to point out. She accompanied her statement with fluttering eyelashes and lots of loud kissing noises, but her teasing died out as soon as we were hit with the full splendor of Heaven.

"This is amazing," Ivy gasped.

A circular, three-hundred-sixty degree bar sat at the center of the room, lit up by an array of magic lights that changed color every few seconds. All around the bar island, the multi-tier dance floor stretched to the far corners of the room. There were people dancing on the ground, on the platforms, and even on the stairs that led up to the second level. I knew most of them had to be members of the Legion, but no one was wearing a uniform today. They were dressed just as Ivy and I were.

Well, maybe not *entirely* as we were. Ivy had missed her calling as a fashionista. She'd put me in a green halter top that made my pale hair stand out beautifully against it. I was wearing it down tonight. Usually super-straight, Ivy had styled it until it took on a waved bounce. My skirt was black and mini, short enough to be flirtatious without degrading into obscene. My boots were over-the-knee, sleek and sexy and comfortable enough to walk in—or to dance in.

Ivy wore a tiny black sleeveless mini dress and a silver gemstone necklace. Her crimson hair, parted on the side, bounced with enviable volume as she walked to the bar with me in her silver sandals. We'd only just sat down when a man in a very suave jacket swooped in and asked her to dance. She gave me an excited wave as she followed him onto the dance floor.

Smiling, I ordered a pineapple juice. When I turned back to look across the dance floor, I was surprised to find Nero sitting beside me.

"You have got to stop doing that," I told him.

"Doing what?"

"Sneaking up on people."

"If you opened up your senses, you would notice your surroundings better," he replied.

Ouch. A lecture. Really? Then again, I wasn't surprised. This was Colonel Hard Ass after all. He was the only one in the whole club wearing a uniform. He probably didn't believe in winding down.

"Wow, this is fun." I drank down my pineapple juice, wishing I'd ordered something harder. "Are you here to let your hair down, Colonel?"

"No."

Ok, then. "Harker talked to me."

"About the blood," he said.

"Yes. He said it's a big no-no according to the Legion."

"It is frowned upon."

"But not forbidden."

"No," he agreed. "The Legion recognizes that its members are human and have needs."

Of course. The ability wasn't called Vampire's Kiss for nothing.

"I knew you were human under all those feathers," I said, grinning at him.

"Yes."

"Harker says you're fighting your inner darkness."

He leaned in closer, his voice dipping. "We all—each of us touched by magic—are fighting that darkness. With me…it's stronger."

"Because you are an angel?"

"Because of who I was before," he said. "My father was an angel. A fallen angel." He paused to let that sink in.

Sometimes angels went bad and joined the demons. Sometimes they went crazy and set off on mad killing sprees. I wondered which kind Nero's father was.

"My mother was also an angel of the Legion."

Wow. There were a few people with one angel parent, but I'd never met one with two. It was no wonder Nero was so powerful.

"When my father went rogue, they assigned my mother to hunt him down," he said.

"She hunted the man she loved?" I asked.

"She hunted him because she loved him. And because she loved me," he said. "My father came for me one night and tried to take me away. My mother fought him. He killed her right in front of my eyes."

I set my hand on his arm. "I'm so sorry."

"I was too angry for sorrow. I ran at my father. I fought him. And I killed him."

"You killed an angel?"

"He'd already been severely weakened by his fight with my mother. Otherwise, I never could have done it. As it was, I was lucky. I knew even then that if I didn't kill him, he would kill me."

"How old were you?"

"Ten."

"I cannot imagine what that must have been like."

"That day, that moment, marked me for life. It made

me who I am today."

I didn't know what to say.

"What doesn't kill you will make you stronger," he told me for only the two millionth time. It was one of his favorite lines. "You must learn to keep going, to have a willpower that doesn't die."

"I am pretty stubborn."

"I see something in you." He met my eyes, and it was as though I could look through to his soul—to see his pain behind the wall he'd built up around himself. "I don't know what it is. That same darkness that I have in me maybe. Being stubborn isn't enough. You also need to learn to control the urges that plague us all."

"Why do you care? I thought you wanted to expose all my secrets."

"I am a patient man. If you die now because you're not strong enough or you succumb to the bloodlust, then I will never find out."

I laughed, lifting my glass to him. We sat there in silence as I watched Ivy. She was dancing with three guys at once. Something about seeing her undiluted happiness made me bold. Or maybe it was the fact that Nero had just spilled his soul to me.

"Want to dance?" I asked him.

He looked at me for a moment, clearly torn. Prudence won out. "I don't think that would be appropriate." He stood. "I must go."

Then without another word, he walked across the room to join Captain Somerset. And I just watched him like an idiot.

"I've been wondering what's between them," Harker said as he sat down beside me. He grinned. "Neither one will admit a thing."

"Oh?"

I was trying not to let that bother me. What did I care if Nero liked someone else? It's not like he was good for me. I suppressed a shudder as I remembered the vicious way he'd torn up the vampires back in that castle. I was *not* going to fall for the bad boy. Not this time. It only ever ended in heartache.

"Come on," Harker said, taking my hand. "Let's dance."

Harker was clearly not worried about what was 'appropriate', and he wasn't trying to slowly kill me. Plus, he had a body to die for, a soul of pure kindness, and he actually knew how to have a good time. He didn't put on his uniform to go to a club. He was wearing dark jeans and a fitted black shirt with translucent black short sleeves. The front zipper was slid down just far enough to hint at the rock-hard physique beneath.

"I'm glad you could come," he said as he set his hands on my hips.

"I was beginning to think *you* wouldn't come."

"Oh, I wouldn't miss it, not if you might be here."

I blushed. Harker was handsome and so human, so approachable. And he really cared about me. I could have an actual conversation with him, one that didn't immediately deteriorate into a verbal sparring match.

"You look beautiful tonight, Leda." He lifted his hand to brush a strand of hair from my face.

"Thanks." I blushed again. "You look nice too."

His hand curled around my back. "Come on. I want to show you something."

His arm wrapped around me, he led me from the dance floor and up the winding staircase into an opulent lounge of lush sofas and antique carpets. I paused at the top to look over the handrails at the flashing and pulsing scene below.

Harker's hand slid around mine. His smile widening, he moved us onto one of the sofas. Most of the others were already occupied. Groups small and large filled them, talking and laughing and dripping tiny glowing drops into one another's mouths.

"What are those drops?" I asked Harker.

"Just a little magical something to help people unwind," he said. "Life at the Legion is tough, full of hard battles. We stare death in the face almost every day. If we don't wind down every so often, we explode."

"Does Nero ever wind down?" I asked. The words just came out.

I regretted it immediately as disappointment crinkled Harker's brow. I was here with him. I shouldn't be dwelling on Nero.

"Nero doesn't unwind," Harker answered despite his disappointment, thereby proving he was a better person than I'd ever be. "That's his problem. That's why he loses control sometimes. I hope you won't make the same mistake." He lifted the vial with the glowing liquid to me.

I stole a glance at the sofa across the aisle from us. Ivy sat there with one of the men she'd danced with downstairs. She opened her mouth, and as he poured a single drop onto her tongue, a look of pure rapture spread across her face. She looked so happy, so free. I yearned for a moment like that, a moment of pure happiness in this dark world. I turned back to Harker, opening my mouth.

A satisfied grin stretched his lips. "Good."

The liquid hit my tongue, a drop of ecstasy exploding inside my mouth. Dizzy with magic and the unraveling strands of my own mind, I swayed to the side. Harker's hands caught my arms, leaning me against the back of the sofa.

"Whoa, there," he said. "You're sensitive for a first-timer."

"The effect grows more intense with time?"

"As your magic level grows." His lips were only inches from mine.

"More please."

He chuckled, low and sexy. "You're adventurous, aren't you?"

He poured a few drops into his own mouth, then gave me two more. Lightning flashed across my body, liquid and hot. Through the cloud of euphoria, I saw Ivy climb onto the man's lap, moaning as he bit her.

Harker brushed his hand across my cheek, returning my attention to him. "Leda," he said, his voice thick, deep.

"Yes?"

"I have a confession to make." His mouth dipped to my neck, trailing a line of burning kisses across my skin.

My head was swimming. "Oh?"

"I'm not the man you think I am." His hand slid up my leg, catching on the hemline of my skirt. "I'm not selfless and kind."

"I'm sure that's not true."

"Oh, but it is. I haven't been helping you all this time because I'm good. I was helping you for my own selfish reasons. I wanted you to like me."

"I do like you." I gasped as his fangs traced up my neck.

"How much do you like me?" he asked, teasing my pulsing, throbbing vein between his teeth.

"Oh, gods, just bite me already, or I'll bite you."

He looked at me, a silver sheen sliding across his blue eyes. "As the lady commands."

Harker dipped his mouth again, but before his fangs could break my skin, a fist flashed before my eyes, knocking him off of me. I snapped my head around to find Nero standing over us.

Harker jumped to his feet, his eyes alight with magic. "You're spoiling my fun, Nero."

"What the hell do you think you're doing?" Nero ground out, cold and cruel.

"Showing the lady a good time. Something you were apparently unwilling to do."

Nero's jaw clenched up, and it was then, as I blinked back the effects of the magic drops, that I realized what was going on all around me. No one was watching us, despite the big scene Nero and Harker were making. The other sofas' occupants were too busy biting one another and making out. Dear gods.

I stumbled to my feet, trying not to trip over them. My head was swirling with a thousand twirling lights. "What is in those drops?" I demanded, looking at Harker.

"Nectar. Diluted down," he added quickly. Guiltily?

"You saw her strong reaction to it before. You shouldn't have given her more," Nero said, anger humming against his cool facade.

"Her reaction? You mean how she bit you and would have had her way with you if I hadn't stepped in." Harker laughed humorlessly. "Yeah, I saw that all right. I saw how you didn't even try to stop her. You wanted her. And you think you have the right to judge *me*? At least I gave her a choice of whether to take the drops instead of pouring it down her throat."

"That was part of the initiation ceremony," Nero said coolly. "And if you weren't so high on Nectar, you would realize that."

"You're not the epitome of sobriety yourself," replied Harker.

I looked at Nero, surprise hitting me when I realized Harker was right. Nero's pupils were dilated. He'd sampled the Nectar tonight too. What had driven Mr. Straight-and-Narrow to do such a thing?

"I found myself in need of calming down," he told me.

Oops. Had I asked myself that out loud? I really needed to stay away from that Nectar.

"Why? Calm down about what?" I asked. I just couldn't stop talking.

Nero's eyes flickered from Harker to me. Oh. He didn't like that we were hanging out. I wasn't even sure what to think about it. It's not like Nero had wanted to hang out with me. *He* had walked away from me.

"Are you all right, Leda?" Nero asked me.

"I'm fine."

"Good."

He spun around and punched Harker. They rolled and kicked and grappled like there was no tomorrow. Their fight finally drew the attention of the drop-licking, blood-sucking, lip-locked people all around us.

Nero tackled Harker against the handrail. Harker grabbed him, pulling and heaving. The two men fell over the barrier, spilling down into the club below. I ran for the stairs, but they were already up and fighting again. Their punches were sharp, their kicks crisp. Every movement was pure perfection. It was like watching two masters at their best.

If only they hadn't been trying to kill each other.

As soon as the fight had landed down below, everyone had scrambled to the edges of the dance floor. They were watching Nero and Harker with a mix of fear and awe.

Neither of them was in his right mind right now, thanks to the Nectar. Someone had to stop them before one of them killed the other. I looked around for this special *someone*, but no one looked prepared to step into the middle of the brawl.

I ran down the stairs, trying to settle my scrambled mind as I hurried toward them. I cut through the air of raging male hormones and magic-induced insanity, planting myself right between them. For one terrifying moment, I feared they wouldn't stop, that they'd plow right through me in their mission to tear each other apart. But they did stop.

"What the hell are you doing?!" I demanded, my voice echoing through the silent room. I almost cringed at the volume of my own voice, but I couldn't afford to show any weakness now. I needed to hold my ground.

"Get out of the way, Leda," Nero said, the timbre of his voice a warning to one and all that they'd best turn around and run for their lives now.

One by one, the people all around us did just that. The club emptied. Soon it was just me and the raging twins. If I'd known what was best for me, I would have left too and just let them fight to the death. But I couldn't do that. I was pissed off as hell at the pair of them right now, but I did not want either of them to die.

"You two need to get your heads on straight," I told them, my eyes burning with anger. They'd probably taken on that creepy silver-blue glow too. Good. It would show them I meant business.

Or maybe not. They continued to glare at each other through me. I had the feeling that if I took just one step back, they'd start going at it again.

"You are best friends," I reminded them. "You do not

want to kill each other. And especially not over who drugged me first or more or whatever. I am a big girl, and I can take care of myself. And I *will* take care of the two of you if you don't stand down this instant."

Nero snorted. "She actually believes she could take us both on," he told Harker.

"Of course she does." Harker grinned. "She's optimistic."

"Delusional rather."

"That too."

They chuckled at my expense, but at least they were lowering their fists. I watched them exchange a silent glance, then walk off together toward the exit.

"You two aren't going off to kill each other, are you?" I called out after them.

"Go home, Pandora," Nero called back, a hint of amusement touching his tone. "Tomorrow morning training starts anew."

Oh goody.

CHAPTER FIFTEEN
The Wicked Wilds

WHEN I WOKE up the next morning, Ivy was just coming into the dormitory, still dressed in her minidress.

"Did you stay up all night?" I asked her, noting her tired eyes and the slightly ruffled state of her dress.

"Well, not *all* night." She tossed her purse onto the dresser. "But close enough. After that little show at Heaven, I went with a few guys to another club."

The look she gave me invited me to expand on the incident with Harker and Nero, but I wasn't up to the invitation today.

Ivy sighed. "Today is going to be hell," she declared as she changed into her sports clothes.

"Like all days here."

Dressed for another day of torture, we headed down to the canteen. Demeter was packed this morning, and the sun hadn't even risen yet. We piled carbohydrates onto our food trays, then went to sit down.

For the first five minutes, Ivy watched me show my stack of pancakes who was boss. She looked like she wanted to say something, but she always caught herself at the last second. Finally, she couldn't hold it in any longer.

"I saw what happened at Heaven last night," she told me.

Her eyes flickered to Nero and Harker, who were sitting at their special table with all the other special snowflakes of the Legion. From the way that they weren't trying to kill each other, I figured they were back on friendly terms.

Ivy grinned at me. "Nero and Harker fought over you."

"That is *not* what happened."

Ivy lifted her fork, pointing it at me. "Darling, that is exactly what happened."

"They were drugged."

She snorted. "Mr. Regulation was high?"

"I saw it in his eyes. And Harker was too." I poked my fruit salad so I wouldn't have to meet her knowing smile.

"You know, the drugs just brought out their baser instincts," Ivy told me. "Harker isn't hiding his intentions, but Nero tries to, though anyone can see he has the hots for you."

"He left me at the bar to talk to Captain Somerset."

"Yeah, to talk about mission reports, I hear. How romantic." She twirled her fork around in the air. "Besides, she prefers ladies to men."

"How can you possibly know this?"

"I talk to people. Peoples' tongues get real loose under the influence of Nectar."

"How many tongues did you loosen last night?" I asked her.

"More than a few."

"You got pretty loose yourself," I teased her.

"I needed to unwind too," she said, winking. "All the Legion soldiers are drinking Nectar during their off time."

"I see. So the Legion of Angels is a legion of drug addicts."

"As long as it doesn't interfere with their job, the gods don't care. In fact, they encourage it. They know their soldiers need to unwind. Someone needs to tell your boy Nero that. He is always so tense. Except last night. I wonder how many drops he had to take before he loosened up enough to punch Harker."

I sighed.

"Those drops were heaven," Ivy said, a dreamy expression washing over her face.

Not as heavenly as Nero's blood. No, I couldn't think about that, about that knee-melting, ecstasy-inducing experience that was drinking his blood. I dug my fingernails into my palms and clung to denial for dear life.

"So, which one do you like?" Ivy asked me.

"I'm trying not to think."

Ivy nodded. "Going with your heart then."

That's not what I'd meant. I was just trying not to think about the whole situation. I couldn't be with either one of them anyway. I was pretty sure the Legion had rules about dating your superiors. They had rules for *everything*. And besides, I had bigger things to worry about. Like Zane. I had to focus on Zane. Not on playing footsie with the major and the colonel.

We finished our breakfast, then headed to the gym. When we got there, Nero was standing with Harker and Captain Somerset. All three were wearing their leather suits. That meant trouble.

"Field trip today," Harker declared cheerfully.

Nero was more subdued. "We're breaking you into three teams. Each team will infiltrate a hideout at a different location we believe rogue vampires to be hiding. It's day, so they should be sleeping and weaker. This mission shouldn't be a problem for you."

Nero's reality meter was way out of whack if he thought bursting into a fortress of angry, self-deprived vampires was 'no problem'. I didn't say anything, though. Trying to reason with Nero was like talking to a wall—except the wall was less stubborn.

The teams were assigned, and I ended up with Ivy and Drake on Captain Somerset's team.

"You're with me, Pandora," she said as the others filed out. She threw a quick glance at Nero and Harker. "It's better this way. The boys need a chance to cool off. We wouldn't want them to start fighting over you again."

I'd told Ivy that they hadn't been fighting over me, but I couldn't argue with Captain Somerset about it. First of all, she was my superior officer, and I really needed to start behaving myself if I was going to make it up the ranks and gain the ability I needed to save Zane. And second of all, I wasn't completely sure she wasn't right.

"How do we know about this hideout?" I asked. That's me. Pure business all the way. "Was this information from the vampire prisoners we captured?"

Captain Somerset gave me a hard, long look. "Nero is right. You ask too many questions."

I pressed on, undeterred. "They wouldn't give up information so easily."

"No one said it was easy, peaches."

"We could be walking into a trap."

"You think too much for your position. That's going to get you into a lot of trouble." A smirk twisted her lips. "But you have a nice ass. That must get you out of a lot of trouble. I can see why Nero and Harker both want to have sex with you."

My mouth dropped in shock at her bluntness.

"Never been with a soldier of the Legion?" she asked,

still grinning. "No worries. I'm sure they'll break you in gently. But you might want to make sure they lay off the drugs before. It tends to make the boys lose control."

"And the girls?" I asked. I could not *believe* I was even having this conversation. This was like some alternate reality or something.

"We are more disciplined." She winked at me.

"There won't be any sex," I stated.

That elicited a chuckle from the captain. "See, I've been around the Legion long enough to know that's just not true. This isn't the first time this has happened."

"That they've come to blows over a woman?"

"Ok, so this is the first time *that* has happened. But many women have come and gone and had their hearts broken by one or both of those two."

"It sounds lovely," I said drily.

"I'm told it is. Up to the inevitable heartbreak, at least. Before then, they enjoyed themselves very much. Nero is an angel, and angels make great lovers. I've had a few myself." She took a moment to savor some fond memory. "And Harker. Well, he's almost an angel. Rumor has it he's next in line to become one, just like he's always wanted. Between the two of them, they must have had a few hundred women."

"Now I *know* you're pulling my leg."

She shrugged. "Immortality is a long time."

When did a soldier of the Legion gain that little ability? Vampires were immortal, and I'd gained their powers. Was I already, unknowingly, immortal too? Would I never age? I tried not to think about it. Immortal or not, a Legion soldier was destined to die young. I tried not to think about that either.

"I've seen them with the same woman," Captain

Somerset continued. "But I've never seen them fight over one." She looked me over. "You're pretty. But I wonder what about you incites the madness in them."

"I'm pretty sure that was the drugs."

She laughed. "You sweet, innocent girl. The drugs merely brought to the surface what was already there." Her eyes narrowed. "I really wonder. What is it about you?"

"I'm told my stubbornness is very endearing."

She snorted. "Nero said that, did he? He's such a hoot. But I don't think that's it. He's drawn to your darkness. And Harker… I think he's drawn to the opposite. To your innocence. To the light inside of you."

"That doesn't make any sense. They can't be drawn to me for opposite reasons. I can't have both darkness and light."

"Who told you that?" she asked, amused.

"The Pilgrims back home were pretty adamant that light can only exist inside of you once you purge the darkness."

She clicked her tongue. "The Pilgrims. They mean well, but their understanding is limited to books, not life. We are all of us a blend of darkness and light. Sometimes the scales are tilted one way, sometimes the other. Even the brightest soul has touches and hints of shadow. And even the darkest soul has seen the light. In the Legion, we take dark and light powers into us. It's how we use them that matters. That is what makes us good or evil. And you." She nodded. "Yes, I see it now. You have both darkness and light in you already, a perfect balance. It's kind of beautiful." She winked at me. "If you ever get sick of those boys, come pay me a visit."

Then she turned and walked out of the room, leaving me rushing to follow.

◆ ◇ ◆ ◇ ◆

We took the train to Montreal, an hour's ride thanks to the engineered magic of Magitech. By car, the trip would have taken hours. This time, no one threw up on the train. That was a victory in and of itself.

Plus Ivy and Drake were on my team. We passed the train ride playing rummy while laughing over all new Legion stories Ivy had learned during her adventure last night.

The rest of our team was made up of three Legion brats: Mina, Roden, and Kinley. Except they weren't acting like brats today. In fact, they didn't bother us at all. Maybe they weren't brats anymore.

When I whispered something to that effect to my friends, Drake said, "They respect you, Leda. And after how you went off alone, braving the Black Plains to bring Nero back, how could they not? The story of your grand rescue is spreading across the Legion."

"So is what happened at Heaven last night," Ivy added, smiling over her cards.

"Ok, what happened last night?" Drake asked. "I heard demons attacked and Nero and Harker blew up an entire city block fighting them off."

"That would have been preferable to what really happened," I muttered.

"Which is?"

Ivy nudged me in my shoulder. "What are you talking about? What really happened was *way* better than demons attacking New York." She looked at Drake. "Harker and Nero were fighting over Leda."

Drake nodded. "Ah, that makes much more sense."

"None of this makes sense. At all," I declared.

The train was just pulling into the station, so we put away our cards. As soon as we stopped, Captain Somerset opened the door, and we all followed her out. Our presence—and Legion uniforms—attracted just as much attention here as it had in Purgatory.

So to the delight of our enthralled audience, we made our way down the street to the Legion office. The one here was a bit bigger than the one back in my hometown—two rooms instead of one—but we were also on the Frontier here. That meant resources were scarce, saved up and devoted to the big wall at the edge of town. After all, that was all that stood between humanity and the monsters.

There were two Legion trucks parked in the garage, and Captain Somerset selected the white one. Then she tossed the keys to Mina.

"I heard you did a good job driving that load of vampires back from the Black Plains, so I'm assigning you as our driver. Try not to crash the truck." She smirked.

There wasn't much to crash into, I thought as we left town. Past the wall, the Wilds—or the Wicked Wilds as many people called them—were nothing but an expanse of brown grass between a few mountains. There were no trees in sight. They'd been an early casualty of the monsters' arrival here.

But as we drove further, trees appeared. It started as just a few sparse bushes, but with each passing mile, the trees grew taller and fuller until we were driving on a narrow street between two immense forests. The cloudy sky opened up, and snowflakes fluttered down softly like goose down.

"Snow? In summer?" Ivy asked, looking up in wonder.

"The weather is all out of whack up here," Captain Somerset said.

Up ahead, the forest opened up into a clearing of three buildings. Two of the buildings had long since run into the ground, but the third was still standing. And from the flickers of light shining through the windows, someone was home.

The captain told Mina to stop the truck and turn off the engine. We stalked toward the forest, keeping to the trees. The snow was coming down harder now. It was getting difficult to see through the gusts of flurries whistling across the land. There were no guards, no alarms or traps. Nothing.

"This feels weird," I said as we stopped at the edge of the trees.

"Not giving up, are you?" Captain Somerset replied.

"I just can't shake the feeling that we were led here. The intel about this place came from the vampires we captured on the Black Plains, didn't it?"

"Yes."

"And the intel about the other two fortresses the Legion is checking out right now?"

"Same."

"And we trust it?" I asked.

"Our interrogators are pretty thorough."

I winced.

"I told you that you asked too many questions. Some things you're best not knowing. Like how many people these bloodsuckers killed in New York and since they've left," she told me.

"A lot?"

"It sure wasn't a little. Bodies piled everywhere, their necks snapped, their blood drained."

I swallowed hard.

Her gaze slid to the building before us. "It does look

bigger than we'd expected. Ok, we're going to move in, but I want you to keep your eyes peeled. Keep to the shadows and be careful. We need to scout the place and figure out how many vampires are hiding in there."

We followed her lead, creeping in silence. No vampires jumped out of the snow piling up fast on the ground. Even as we entered the building, nothing happened. The hallways were empty, the rooms abandoned. It felt like a tomb in here.

It *was* a tomb. Our tomb. As we entered the large central chamber, vampires jumped out of the floorboards, fully awake. And they weren't alone. The doors burst open, and witches and werewolves streamed in from the connecting rooms, surrounding us.

CHAPTER SIXTEEN
The Next Generation of Monsters

WHEN FACED WITH a horde of vampires, there was really only one thing you could do. No, not run away screaming like hell. The Legion of Angels frowned upon displays of outright cowardice in its soldiers. So we raised our guns and shot the vampires full of Legion-issued magic tranquilizers. They dropped like flies.

The werewolves didn't react so kindly. In fact, the tranquilizers didn't seem to do anything but make them angry. I kept shooting anything that moved anyway. What else could I do? We weren't armed for anything but vampires.

If it had been *just* the vampires, we would have been ok, even with their numbers. We hadn't counted on the supernatural support squad. What were they doing helping the rogue vampires?

Captain Somerset dashed forward, drawing her freakishly large sword. She slashed and slid, cut and cleaved, tearing through anything that made it past our firing line. I was really glad she was on our side. That woman was frighteningly fierce. And deadly efficient.

But it wasn't enough.

The werewolves were breaking through, and I had no idea what cloud of impending doom the witches were brewing up in the back. I did know that if we didn't take care of it fast, that cloud would escalate beyond impending. The Legion brats already had their knives drawn, and they were holding their own against the shifters. Drake was wrestling with one of the wolves, putting those magic-enhanced football tackling skills to good use.

Ivy and I went for the witches. The cloud was descending on our teammates, along with all kinds of potions the witches were throwing at us.

"We've got to put a stop to that," I told Ivy as a bottled lightning bolt exploded beside my foot.

We moved in, evading firebombs and insect swarms and weird green goo. One of the potion bottles broke right in front of me, splattering my legs with tiny red drops. Those red drops promptly burst into flames all across the leather. Pain permeated the surface of my pants, burning into my skin. I patted out the flames, but the damage was done. I grabbed hold of the witch and sank my fangs into her neck. Drinking her blood wasn't the orgasmic experience drinking Nero's blood had been. Not even close. But it did heal me. I sort of loved the irony of using her blood to heal the damage she'd caused to my body. Her eyes trembled with fear, as though she were afraid I'd drain her dry.

"You don't taste that good," I told her, then shot a tranquilizer into her.

I pivoted, shooting down the rest of the witches around me. A shriek of agony drew my attention across the room. A seven-foot werewolf held Ivy in his claws, his teeth dripping with blood. She had a werewolf-sized bite mark on her arm. When he snapped his jaws at her to take another bite, she punched him in the face. Roaring, he flung her across the room. My friend landed in a limp heap on the floor.

I ran right for her, but a pair of werewolves jumped in my way. I tried to get around them with no success. They were too big and fast. They blocked me at every turn.

"Help Ivy!" I shouted to Drake.

The werewolf who'd thrown her wasn't done with her yet. He raked and clawed at her. Every time she tried to get up, he knocked her back down. She rolled into a ball, protecting her face. Drake was cut off from her by a wall of four werewolves. I had to help her.

I faced down the two wolves in front of me, drawing my knife. I slashed at the first werewolf, but she knocked the knife from my hand. Then both wolves jumped at me. I sidestepped, knowing I was no match for those claws. If they got in a blow, I'd be in even worse shape than Ivy. The werewolves were stronger than I was, and there were two of them.

I evaded them again, diving for my knife lying on the ground. As the first wolf landed, I jammed it up into her paw. She roared, running around wildly on three legs as she cradled her wound. I grabbed Ivy's gun and mine off the floor and unloaded everything I had into the second wolf. *That* knocked him out.

I ran past the limping wolf, who was trying to grip the hilt of the knife in her mouth so she could pull it out. But her mouth was too big and not meant for precision work. She would be busy for a while. Drake had broken through too. His four wolves lay unmoving on the floor, but he was still grappling with the one who'd mauled Ivy. The wolf stood in front of our friend, preventing anyone from getting to her.

Ivy looked bad. She was unconscious with a huge bruise on her head. Her leather suit was torn open, reduced to shreds across her abdomen. She was bleeding out of it all over the floor.

And that damn wolf was not moving. It reared to its back legs and backhanded Drake out of range. I ran at the wolf, picking Ivy's knife off the ground as I moved. I dove under its peddling front legs and stabbed it through the heart. It jerked, trying to knock me off. I held on, even as its blood poured down my arm, making my grip slick. The beast continued to buck and rear. And I continued to dig the knife in deeper, trying to shred its heart. Its claws slashed across my face, drawing blood.

My arms shook and spasmed under the strain of wrestling a five-hundred pound werewolf, but I could not let go. If I did, not only was I dead—so was Ivy. I swung my legs around the wolf, locking them together behind its back. Then I heaved with everything I had to plunge the knife all the way through its heart.

The wolf died, collapsing on top of me. No matter how much I tried to push and wiggle and kick, I could not get him off of me. I tried not to think about the dead person bleeding out all over me—and especially not about the fact that I'd killed him. Instead I focused on breathing. That was starting to get hard. Between the blotches of yellow and purple light. I saw boots clicking by, then stopping beside me. I looked up into the face of Captain Somerset.

"You did well," she told me as I struggled to breathe.

She lifted the beast off of me and threw it aside like it weighed nothing. My jaw would have dropped if it had had any strength left to do so. I rolled over and pushed up to my knees to check on my friend.

"She's not breathing!" I said desperately.

◆ ◇ ◆ ◇ ◆

Captain Somerset got Ivy stabilized. She hadn't yet acquired the gods' gift of healing magic, but she was fully stocked with mega-dose healing potions. As soon as she gave Ivy a few, my friend began to breathe again. We loaded up the truck with the surviving members of the enemy army, then carefully spread Ivy across one of the rows. Drake and I watched over her the whole drive back to town.

Once there, we brought Ivy to the local fairy healer, who patched her up as best he could, but he warned us that her wounds were beyond his magic. We had to get her back to the healers at the Legion building in New York.

We were on the train now, counting down the minutes until we drove into the city. Drake was holding Ivy's hand. Even though she wasn't conscious, I knew she'd have appreciated the gesture anyway. Mina, Roden, and Kinley were standing guard over our prisoners—at least what few we'd managed to catch this time. When we were swarmed, survival had trumped the need for prisoners. I only hoped the Legion saw it the same way. They were funny about things like that.

"Ok, see you in half an hour," Captain Somerset spoke into her phone, then tucked it into her jacket.

I was sitting next to her, eavesdropping on her conversation with Nero and Harker. She hadn't even tried to shoo me away.

"You were right," she told me with a sigh. "The vampires the Legion tortured for these locations knew they were sending us into a trap. The same thing that happened to us happened to Nero's and Harker's groups. This is bigger than vampires being turned outside of the system.

We all infiltrated sites that were supposed to be just vampires, but we each found a lot more."

"Is everyone all right?" I asked.

"There were no casualties on our side," she replied to my great relief. There had been enough death already.

"What's going on?" I asked. "Who is behind this?"

"Demons."

That single word stunned me to silence.

"It's demons," she continued. "And they aren't only turning vampires. They are also turning shifters and getting witches to defect. The bodies we found over the past few days were the people they were unable to turn to their side. They're building an army to challenge the gods."

"Why don't they just use the monsters?" I wondered. "They control them, right?"

Captain Somerset lowered her voice to hardly above a whisper. "No."

"No?" I whispered back.

She leaned in closer. "What I'm going to tell you doesn't leave the Legion. No one can know about it. Not your friends or family. No one."

I nodded.

"In the war of gods and demons, it wasn't just the demons who unleashed the monsters," she said. "The gods and the demons both did. As the war escalated, they bred stronger and more resilient monsters to fight the other side's monsters. But they lost control of them. The beasts would no longer obey their masters' commands. The monsters tore across the Earth, devastating it rather than attacking the other side's army. In the end, the gods won the war. They pushed the demons back to their realm. But it was too late. They and the demons had made the monsters too strong. Too resilient to magic."

"And that's why the gods gave humanity magic," I realized. "That's why they built the wall."

It hadn't been an act of mercy. They were only trying to mitigate the mess that they themselves had made.

"Yes," she said. "The gods needed us to help them rebuild the Earth. Two hundred years later, the battle for this Earth still rages on. What we do here at the Legion is important."

The gods gave us magic and strength that empowered us to slay their enemies. We were the next generation of monsters. And now the demons were trying to build their own next generation of monsters too.

The revelation was troubling—but not surprising. Humans were nothing but tools to the gods, something to be used. Well, I was going to use them right on back to save Zane. Dark angels had taken him, and that meant demons. So I was going to side with the gods. For now. I just wouldn't tell them about Zane.

CHAPTER SEVENTEEN
Perfect Balance

WHEN I ENTERED the Legion's medical ward, I half-expected to find Ivy sitting up, chatting and charming the healers. Instead, I found her asleep and hooked up to an assortment of Magitech machines. The healers assured me that Ivy was just fine, that they'd put her to sleep to allow the magic to fully heal her body, but it was hard to believe them when I walked into *that*. A pink box of cookies from Ivy's mother sat on the table, unopened. I hoped the Legion was at least giving the poor woman regular updates on Ivy's condition. From the frequent care packages she sent her, it was clear that she really loved her daughter.

I left the room, feeling useless and frustrated. Harker caught up with me halfway down the hall. He met my gaze, and I saw pity in his eyes.

"Come on. Let's walk," he said, taking my hand.

As we stepped outside, I caught a glimpse of Nero on the other end of the hallway. He was watching our every move, but he didn't take a step toward us.

Harker waited until we'd passed into the waterlily gardens before he spoke again. "How are you holding up?"

"I'm fine." I rubbed my hands against my arms, trying

to drive out the chill that had taken root in my soul. "I'm not the one who's lying unconscious in the medical ward. Or in a grave." I shuddered.

"This isn't about just our bodies, Leda. It's just as much —no, even *more* so—about our minds. You have never killed anyone before today. But we are soldiers in an army, fighting a war. And in war, there are casualties. People die. That is what soldiers—what *we*—do."

"I've fought people before."

"You've wounded them, you've shot them full of magic tranquilizers. But this is different. The Legion strips away your innocence." He set his steady hands over my shaking ones. "The adrenaline is crashing and you're beginning to process what you've done."

I looked him in the eye, my voice quivering. "What's your point?"

"If you need anyone to talk to, I'm here for you." Then he kissed my forehead and walked away.

I didn't know if I wanted to wallow in sorrow alone or cry on someone's shoulder. So I just stood there, staring across the beautiful pool of white and pink waterlilies spread out before me, and I tried very hard not to think. But try as I might, I could not block out the flood of images flashing through my head, the memories of what I'd done—and the blood on my hands.

"Leda."

I turned around to find Nero standing behind me.

"So," I said, wiping the tears from my cheeks. "Have you too come to see if I'm cracking?"

"No. I know you're not cracking. You're too strong."

I let out a wretched, pained laugh. "No, I'm not."

"This is not the last time you will have to kill," he said. "Nor the last time you will do things you don't like all in the name of the greater good."

"Thanks for the uplifting pep talk."

"I'm not here to sugarcoat anything or lie to you, Leda. It is the way it is. I warned you about this when you joined the Legion."

"So you think I don't belong here?"

"Only you can know that. Everyone who joins the Legion has their reasons. Everyone needs something, something they feel is missing inside of them. Some crave power, some need to serve, some wish to help someone they love."

"Why did you join?" I asked him, my curiosity getting the better of me.

But he didn't look offended by my question. "It was expected of me. I had two Legion soldiers as parents, both of them angels. When my father went rogue and my mother went hunting after him, another angel, a friend of theirs, took me in. He trained me. And he continued to do so after my parents died. He molded me into what I was supposed to be: the perfect Legion soldier. After I joined, I climbed the ranks quickly, more quickly than anyone ever had. I had been made for nothing else."

"That's kind of sad."

"You feel sorry for me. Don't. I was broken after my parents died. This angel, then the Legion, gave me purpose. That was my need. That is the hole the Legion filled inside of me."

"You don't ever feel like you never had a choice, that your life was never yours?" I asked him.

"We are all pawns in this world. Choice is an illusion."

"I don't believe that."

"Really?" A single eyebrow arched upward at me. "What were you doing before you joined the Legion?"

"Working as a bounty hunter."

"For your foster mother," he said. "Why did you choose that job?"

"My family needed me. And I was good at my job."

"Because Callista groomed you for exactly that job. Just as I was groomed for the Legion."

I shook my head. "It's not the same at all."

"And what about before that?" he asked, ignoring my protest. "Where were you before Callista found you?"

"Living on the streets."

"That explains your scrappy fighting." Amusement quirked his lower lip. "And why were you on the streets?"

"Because my previous foster mother died, killed by the gang who robbed her."

"And your parents?"

"They died when I was a baby. I never knew them."

"You've had a lot of loss in your life, a lot of pain. It made you strong. It made you resilient. It gave you that stubborn tenacity the Legion needs in its soldiers. Everything in your life led up to the day you joined the Legion."

"No," I said, denial springing to my lips. "That was a choice. I chose to come here. I chose to join the Legion."

"Something prompted you to come. I don't know what it is." He looked into my eyes, as though he could read the story of my life in them. "Compassion. You're here for someone. You don't crave power, and you have too much of an independent mind to feel compelled to serve the gods."

I didn't speak, not wanting to give anything away.

He shook his head. "But it's not important. Something happened, and someone you care about needs you. You're gaining powers to help this person. It's not all that uncommon, though less common than the need for power or affirmation. I can tell you that people with your motivation tend to make it further than others."

"Now that's more like a pep talk," I teased him.

But he would not be deterred from this path. "Whoever prompted you to join the Legion is not important. If it hadn't been that person, it would have been another. One thing or another would have eventually led you to our doors."

"You sound awfully sure that I'm destined to be here."

"Yes. It's who you are," he said simply.

"Then why did you not want me to join?" I asked.

"I saw an innocence in you." He set his hands on my cheeks. "A beautiful innocence. The Legion strips away our innocence. It makes us hard. It makes us less human. I didn't want to see that happen to you."

"And yet you agreed to let me join."

He leaned in, his hand brushing against mine. "I realized it was inevitable. The way you fought those vampires, three of them against just one of you. I saw your tenacity, that you weren't going to give up, that one way or another you would join the Legion."

"Do you wish I weren't here?" I asked quietly.

He laughed. "You must think me very selfless."

"That's not an answer."

"You have changed this place, Leda. Your passion, your stubbornness, your humanity, even that attitude of yours."

He brushed his fingers across my lip, stirring memories of the last time we'd been this close, of his blood in me. And mine in him. My mouth throbbed, and I struggled to push back my emerging fangs.

"Captain Somerset says you are drawn to the darkness inside of me," I said.

Nero laughed. "I'll have to have words with Basanti

about her betrayal. Yes, I'm drawn to your darkness. It is my dark side that seeks the darkness. But how I feel about you…it's not like she thinks."

"So it's not my impeccable behavior and deep respect for authority?"

His laugh was both sharp and sexy. "I'm afraid not."

"Good. Because those things are really boring."

"There is nothing boring about you, Leda, nothing typical. You are in perfect balance: light and darkness. You prove that both can exist in harmony inside of one person. That one does not have to consume the other. People of light often are arrogant and self-righteous. But you are neither. Just as you do not take pleasure in losing control, in excess, in pain as those ruled by darkness do. For so long, it's been a battle between light and darkness, between gods and demons. We're forced to pick one or the other. We all fall somewhere on that scale of darkness and light, but none of us are balanced. Except you."

"You can see this?" I asked.

"I can feel it, yes. The gods would call it blasphemy, the demons madness, but I think your perfect balance is the most beautiful thing I've ever seen. You, Leda. You make me feel like there is hope for humanity, for all of us."

He dipped his mouth to kiss me on the cheek, then he walked away, leaving me still whirling with the most romantic speech I'd ever heard. I stood there for a while, my mind trying to sort through everything Harker and Nero had said. It finally gave up trying to resolve my conflicted feelings about them—and about myself. I returned to my dormitory.

I'd been gone so long that the healers had transferred Ivy in that time to our room. She was awake and happy and healed. She and Drake sat crosslegged on her bed, the now-open box of cookies wedged between them.

"I'm sorry," I said guiltily, sitting down beside them. "I got held up. I wasn't here to welcome you back."

"You don't ever have to apologize to me, Leda." She hugged me. "You saved my life."

"Drake might have helped a little," I said, squeezing my thumb and index finger together.

Ivy and I laughed.

"That's right. Laugh all you want," he said, nodding. "But don't you come to me the next time you have werewolves that need tackling."

"Do we expect this to be a regular occurrence?" Ivy asked.

"This is the Legion of Angels, not the Girl Scouts," Drake told her.

"Well, I'm still keeping my cookies." As she reached into the box, a silver bracelet with a tiny charm slid down over her wrist.

I blinked, clearing my vision. I'd seen the symbol on that charm before.

"How long have you had that bracelet?" I asked her.

"Awhile. I don't often wear it, but I put it on because it's supposed to speed my healing by cleansing my aura." She shrugged. "At least that's what my mom says. She made it for me a few years ago."

"What is that symbol?"

"I'm not sure. It's my mother's symbol."

"I've seen it before." I stared at that symbol of a flower of never-ending layers, the symbol I'd seen painted on the door of the ghost's shop.

"What's wrong?" Ivy asked me.

Everything. "Do you have a picture of your mother?"

"Sure."

Ivy pulled one up on her phone and showed me the screen. The face of Calli's friend Rose stared back at me.

"Leda?"

"I know her." I swallowed hard. "And I saw her die."

"That's impossible," Ivy protested. "She's been writing to me since I came here. I've even spoken to her a few times."

I grew very cold as the world clicked into focus, as I realized what was going on.

"Your mother is working for the demons," I told my friend.

CHAPTER EIGHTEEN
Sweet Dreams

"THAT'S NOT FUNNY, Leda," Ivy said, furrowing her brows.

I pointed at the photo on her phone. "I saw that woman die in front of my eyes."

"That's impossible."

"Your mother is named Rose," I told her. "She runs a cheesy psychic readings shop in the city, but she is the real deal. She's a telepath—a ghost—but she's been hiding her gift because if the gods found out about her, they would take her away."

Ivy's mouth dropped. "How can you possibly know about that?"

"I know because your mom is friends with my foster mother Calli. And because when we paid her a visit in New York, we found her dying in a pool of her own blood. She said a dark angel attacked her." I shook my head. "No, something else is going on here. You petitioned the Legion to heal your mother's cancer by turning her into a vampire. When your petition was rejected, she must have taken matters into her own hands. She made a deal with the demons. In exchange for them healing her, she agreed to help them."

"Help them do what?" Drake asked.

"Build a demon army. And... Oh, shit." I bounced off the bed, jumping to my feet. "I have to go. Take care of Ivy," I told Drake as I hurried toward the door. "I'll be back."

I ran out of the room and to the stairwell. I took the stairs two at a time, rushing higher and higher. The higher ranked officers of the Legion had their rooms on the top level of the building. Whatever was going on in this war between gods and demons, it went deep. Rose had been turned to their side. What if some of the Legion had too? I had to bring this to the top, to Nero. He couldn't have been turned. The angel was a stickler for regulations and protocol. To him, disloyalty was a four-letter word. With exclamation points.

Sucking in hot, heaving breaths, I burst into the hallway on the top floor. I ran past doors neatly marked with each officer's name, silently thanking the Legion for their overly-developed organization skills. Near the end of the hallway I found a door that read 'Colonel Nero Windstriker'. I knocked on it twice, nice and calm. Half a minute passed—and so did a pair of captains who shot me harsh looks—but Nero didn't answer. I'd just lifted my fist to knock again when the door across the hall opened and Harker stepped out.

"Leda?" He froze as his eyes met mine, taking in my ruffled appearance. "What's wrong?"

"I need to speak to Nero. About the mission," I added quickly as disappointment flashed in his eyes.

"He had to leave the city," Harker said. "He's leading another raid on a potential rogue vampire site."

What wretched timing.

"Maybe I can help you," Harker said. "I'm in charge until Nero returns."

I glanced up and down the hall, my mouth tightening. He seemed to realize I was feeling really paranoid about eavesdroppers at the moment because he pushed his door wide open and motioned me forward.

"Please come in," he said.

I took him up on his offer, following him into his room—no *apartment*, I realized as I entered a living room that was larger than the dormitory room I shared with five other people. The floors were oak, the windows floor-to-ceiling, and the furniture looked like it belonged in a castle. There were two doors off to the side of the living room. I saw a large canopy bed in one and an in-floor hot tub in the other. Making it high in the Legion certainly had its perks.

But I didn't have time to stop and admire the opulence. I turned to Harker, who was looking at me like I'd cracked.

"I want to help you, Leda," he said. "Are you struggling with what happened in the Wilds?"

"What?" I asked, confused until I realized he was talking about the werewolf I'd killed. "No, it's not that. It's something else."

He waited for me to talk, keeping his distance as though he realized I needed my pacing room.

"What if I told you I had a lead on a rogue vampire site inside the city, one that might lead us back to the demons?"

His face was carefully neutral. "How do you know this?"

"It's just a hunch," I said. "It might not pan out. But if it does…"

"We could wipe out the demons' operation in the city." He nodded. "We cannot allow them to gain a foothold into our world. What do you know?"

I hesitated.

"Leda, you are a soldier of the Legion of Angels. You have sworn to protect this Earth and its people from the demons and monsters. I can help you, but you have to trust me."

I chewed on my lip, thinking it over. "Ok." I summarized what I knew about Rose and her deal with the demons, leaving out the part with my brother of course. My first loyalty was still to Zane, Legion or no Legion.

Harker listened to me speak, the perfect audience.

"Ivy's mother was turned by the vampires, the ones working for the demons," I finished. "If we find her, we'll find the demons."

"She works for them," he said, frowning as though the idea tasted bitter on his tongue.

"She was dying. In pain. Suffering," I defended her. "It's not her fault. We have to save her, not harm her."

Harker stared at me for a moment, as though he were trying to read my intentions in my eyes. "Ok," he finally said. "Let's do it. We'll save her."

"Thank you."

"We learn to deal out punishment here. But we also learn mercy."

I rushed forward, closing the distance between us to hug him. "We can't tell anyone in the Legion. They would make Rose suffer for what she's done."

I expected him to argue, to tell me I was asking the impossible, but he just said, "This is just between the two of us."

I squeezed him tightly to me, happy to have discovered that there was something left of humanity after all.

"How will we find her?" he asked me after I let him go.

"With this," I said, showing him the shipping slip I'd

peeled from Ivy's cookie box.

◆ ◇ ◆ ◇ ◆

Harker and I geared up and went to go pay a visit to Deliverance, the shipping company who'd delivered Ivy's cookies. Back when I'd been a bounty hunter scouting for information, I'd had to do things like this really indirectly. You couldn't just walk into the office of the world's largest delivery company and demand to see their shipping records for the last two days. That was, unless you worked for the Legion of Angels. We had the list in under five minutes, along with a hot cup of coffee and a brownie. I could get used to this.

Unfortunately for us, whoever had sent the cookies had used a fake return address. I seriously doubted that the First Paranormal Police Precinct of New York City had sent Ivy a box of sweets. Harker had the Deliverance receptionist call up the delivery guy for that package.

And that's how we ended up here outside of Sweet Dreams, the city's newest bakery. They'd set up shop just a few weeks ago. The delivery guy hadn't known anything more about the shipping records than Deliverance's computer system, but he had recognized the cookie I showed him. That triple chocolate recipe with a sprinkle of fairy's breath was exclusive to one bakery: Sweet Dreams.

Darkness was falling on the city. When we reached the bakery, we found a 'Closed' sign over the door, but there were lights on inside. Harker pulled out a tiny piece of metal the size and shape of a beetle. As soon as he switched on the Magitech, the little bug hopped out of his hand and scuttled under the door to the shop.

We watched its progress from Harker's phone screen,

which allowed us to see everything the bug did. The front area was your typical bakery parlor. Rows of sweets sat behind glass counters. Cookies, muffins, cinnamon rolls…a glass dish of candies and chocolates on the countertop next to the register.

A woman wearing a pink-and-white striped apron stood in front of one of these counters. Opposite her were two young couples, holding hands and looking around like at any moment something might jump out from behind one of the counters and kill them. The apron lady tapped her earpiece, as though she'd just received instructions, then she opened the door into the back area, waving the two couples through.

As they disappeared into the back, we hurried to the front door. Using another piece of Magitech, Harker had it open in two seconds. An aroma of baked sweets and flowers tickled my nose as we stepped quickly but softly across the checkered vinyl floor and followed the procession deeper into the building.

Ahead of us, neither the apron lady nor the couples said a word. The couples were still looking around nervously, as though they expected the gods' wrath to strike them down where they stood. These must have been new recruits to the demons' army. Of course they were nervous if they were about to betray the gods. The gods weren't exactly known for forgiveness.

We passed baking ovens and preparation tables, stoves and supplies. The whole place was very sterile—and very, very creepy.

We passed through another door. This one brought us to an area that looked more like a warehouse than a bakery. The walls were covered in sheets of discolored metal, and the ground squeaked like the floor of a parking garage.

There were storage shelves all around the room, and it was behind one of them that Harker and I hid as the procession in front of us came to a stop.

The apron lady, who I could now smell was a vampire, held a clipboard in front of her. "Marla and Vincent," she said, looking at one of the couples. "It says here that you have been on the waiting list to be turned into vampires for nearly a year. And that Vincent—" She glanced at the man. "Is terminally ill."

"Yes," Marla said, her voice a hard rasp, even parts fear and determination. "He has only months left." She squeezed the man's hand. "And we don't wish to be separated."

"I'm sure we can help you with your problem," the aproned vampire said, then turned to the second couple. "Adara and Jaden. You come from different vampire houses, Adara from House Vermillion and Jaden from House Snowfire. Your lords do not permit unions to vampires outside their walls."

Forbidden love. So what we had here in these two couples was a regular Romeo and Juliet and yet again a few people stuck at the wrong end of a very long vampire waiting list. The demons were building their army from the desperate and disgruntled, people like Rose and these couples. And this bakery was the front for their vampire-turning operation.

"So how does this work exactly?" the vampire Jaden asked nervously.

"My supervisor will arrive shortly to explain everything," the aproned vampire said with a sugar-coated smile.

I wondered if any of them knew what they were getting into. This wasn't just an information evening on The Basics of Insurgence at the friendly local bakery. If they didn't agree to the demons' deal, they wouldn't be walking out of here. Letting anyone go would inevitably lead the Legion to their doorstep.

Except I'd jumped the gun. We were already here. The question was what we were going to do about it. There were only two of us. Harker could easily handle the five of them himself if things turned ugly, but I had a feeling there were more people in this building.

A door opened across the warehouse. Sharp, confident footsteps echoed off the walls as a new arrival strode across the room. As the supervisor came into the light, I realized it wasn't a demon or even another vampire. It was Rose.

"Welcome," she declared with a wide smile as a dozen doors opened all across the warehouse, and vampires poured out, surrounding us.

CHAPTER NINETEEN
Steel and Bones

ROSE WAS COMPLETELY healed. There was not a wound on her. But it wasn't just that. Rose wasn't just in perfect health. She was positively glowing.

"What did the demons give you?" I asked her.

A smile of pure happiness spread across her lips. "Immortality. Just as you at the Legion drink from the gods' Nectar, we have a nectar of our own."

Harker cursed under his breath. I guessed he'd heard of this demon nectar.

"This was the price of your life?" I said to Rose, waving my hand around to indicate this shady operation. "The demons told you they would cure your cancer if you helped them?"

Rose laughed like I'd said the funniest thing in the world. "It was not the demons who came to me. I went to them. This was *my* idea."

She actually looked proud of herself.

"I was never one to take death lying down," she continued. "Never one to play the victim, to let things happen to me. In that way, we are a lot alike, Leda. You would have done the same."

"No," I said, the denial immediate. "You are killing people."

"I am freeing them from the tyranny and meaningless rules that have broken them. Some refused, blinded by their devotion to a broken system. They were polluting the positive energy of our new order, so they had to be dealt with. But most people embraced the change." Rose indicated the two couples. "Look at them. Forlorn, suffering, without hope. I am giving them hope and new life. I founded this house. At first, it was about curing me, but now it's grown into so much more. We are free here."

"No, you're not," I told her. "You've just traded one master for another. You are nothing but a pawn in this game of gods and demons. The demons are using you to build their army. Why can't you see that?"

"I am free to choose. This was my plan. My idea."

I shook my head. There was just no getting through to her. She'd buried herself inside a mountain of denial so high that she couldn't even see the truth anymore.

"It was a foolish plan," Harker told her. "The gods always find out."

"You foolish, mindless soldier." She looked at him with more pity than malice. "You were all running around helplessly, confused. You're so stuck on your devotion to your gods that you couldn't even fathom anyone would move against them. And ignorant you would have remained." She shot me an irked look. "If not for you, Leda. How did you know I was still alive?"

"Ivy's bracelet. The charm has the same symbol as on your shop's door."

She sighed. "My dear daughter. I never expected her to join the Legion."

"She was trying to save *you*."

"And she would have been too late. I wouldn't have survived the first month. But it was a noble gesture." She favored me with a kind smile. She actually seemed to like me. "Noble like you, dear. And what you're doing for your brother."

Harker looked at me.

A ghost of a smile kissed her lips. "You haven't told him? Or Nero? The two boys who fought over you."

I glowered at her. "You know an awful lot about what's going on at the Legion."

"Ivy wrote to me. She told me stories. We've always been close."

"She will be heartbroken when she realizes she doesn't know you at all."

"You care about her. Good. She will need a friend in the hard days to come."

Rose waved to her army of vampires, and they attacked Harker. Every step, every punch and slash, led him further from me. The vampires were breaking us apart. But they weren't even attacking me. They were concentrating all their attention on him. He was holding them off, but there were just so many of them. I drew my gun to help him.

"Stop," Rose said. "If you die, you will never find your brother. No one will."

I paused, torn between two impossible decisions. Harker made the choice for me. He lifted his fist into the air, expelling a wave of psychic magic that shot the vampires to the far edges of the room.

"I sent you to the Legion for a reason," she told me. "Don't squander your chance to save your brother."

"You were working with her?" Shock washed across Harker's face—shock and betrayal.

"Of course not. My mom knows her," I told him "We

went to her for...for some help finding my brother. We found her bleeding on the floor. She was dying." A realization hit me, dropping like a cold, hard rock into the pit of my stomach. "A dark angel didn't attack you," I said to Rose.

"Oh, he attacked me all right. Those wounds weren't fake."

"But it *was* staged. So, you...you could get me to join the Legion." I frowned. "You said it was the only way to save Zane."

"And it is."

"Through Ghost's Whisper," muttered Harker. "That is why you joined the Legion."

There was no point in denying it. "Yes."

He was quiet for a moment, reflective—even as the vampires stuck to the walls struggled against his psychic grip. He flicked his hand, and all of them simultaneously burst into flames. Wow, he really was powerful.

"You are noble," he finally said to me. "I know you will do the right thing."

I didn't even know what the right thing was. I was doing the selfish thing. Zane was my brother, and I loved him and wanted to see him again, so I was going to save him.

"You used me." I glared at Rose. "You wanted me to join the Legion, so I could lead you to Zane. But why? Dark angels took my brother. The demons already have him."

"No," Rose said, that single word a ray of hope in the dark room. "That was someone else."

Had Sheriff Wilder's daughter only thought she'd seen dark angels that night? Had fear and the darkness of night forced her mind to fill in the gaps? Or had someone cast an illusion with magic, someone who didn't want us to know who'd really taken Zane?

"But if the demons don't have Zane, then who does?" I muttered to myself.

"That is something I trust you will find out," Rose said.

A second wave of vampires streamed in through the open doors, surrounding us. Harker drew his sword and charged at them. His magic must have been running too low to repeat the spontaneous combustion trick again. Ignoring Rose's warnings, I jumped into the fray to help him. I shot one of them before he could shoot Harker, then threw another one aside so I could move back-to-back with him.

"I see you've made your decision." Rose's words dripped with disappointment.

"Yeah, I guess I really have," I told her.

Harker and I fought off the vampires together, our movements coordinated, as though we'd practiced this a million times before. Except I hadn't. In fact, I'd never fought this well before, but I could feel him feeding me a little of his magic, of his experience—giving me a little nudge to bring me through the movements like a dancer leading his partner. And we were magnificent.

Until the Legion came.

As our own soldiers poured through the doors, engaging the never-ending stream of Rose's vampires, that strand between me and Harker snapped.

"This was supposed to be between us. You promised you wouldn't tell the Legion," I said, the sting of his betrayal burning my throat.

"Are you really going to be angry about this now?" He shot another vampire. "Right now, they are saving our lives. You can be mad at me later."

He was right, but I was too upset with him to admit it. And too busy to argue with him. I had to stay alive. Rose was right about one thing: if I died, I couldn't save my brother.

So I fought and killed the vampires. Red stained my vision, a combination of blood and anger and that old enemy fear. I didn't slow, and I didn't stop to think about what I was doing. If I stopped, I was dead. The vampires were too fast. Worse yet, the realization of what I was doing—the people I was killing—would cripple me in such a way that not even supernatural speed could make up for it.

Caught in this daze of crimson, I was vaguely aware of Harker beside me, hacking through vampires left and right. Their bodies were piling up everywhere, falling in my path. Bile rose in my throat at the sheer scale of death around me.

Harker broke through the line of vampires, making a run for Rose as she tried to escape. She didn't make it far. He lifted his sword, and in one swift stroke, he cut clear through her neck. Her head thumped to the ground, her body tumbling down a moment later. I froze, paralyzed. Rose was dead. Ivy would be crushed.

That moment of distraction cost me. A vampire grabbed hold of my arm, yanking me toward him as he bit down hard on my neck. Pain bubbled up from the mark his fangs had torn into my flesh. I kicked him in the knee, then hurled him at the wall.

I looked for my next target, but a rush of dizziness made me stumble. Something hot and wet was gushing down my neck. I lifted my hand to my throat to find it torn open and slick with my own blood. That same blood sprinkled down from me, splattering the floor. But I couldn't give up now. The vampires had us outnumbered.

Where were they all coming from? I considered reaching into my jacket for a roll of gauze and trying to bandage up my wound, but a solid thump to my head from a nearby vampire reminded me that I didn't have time for that shit. I'd just have to fight bloody.

My mind was too stubborn to give up, but my body was failing. My vision blurred, my steps swayed. Hands caught me before I hit the ground. I blinked, looking up into Harker's face.

"Leda, gods," he gasped, his eyes widening. "What happened to you?"

I tried to steady myself, to stand on my own two feet, but he held on like I was one step away from falling to pieces. I was too numb to know if he was right. I could hear the clash of steel and the crunch of bones. The fight was still going on, and I should have been in it.

"I'm fine," I insisted, pushing against his stubborn hold. "Let me go."

"You can't fight, Leda. Not in this state."

I blinked several times in quick succession, trying to clear my vision. But darkness was falling, consciousness slipping. I felt a warm pulse of magic encase me like a blanket, and then I passed out.

CHAPTER TWENTY
Magic in a Bottle

I DREAMED I was standing on the battlefield between two warring armies, each side led by angels. Beautiful and terrible, they clashed in a war of magic and might that shook the ground and echoed across the heavens. Swords clashed. Steel clanged. The stench of blood and sulfur and death permeated the air. Feathers fluttered on the wind. The soil was soaked with blood; it spread out from the battlefield, blackening the Earth. The storm of spells raged on.

A woman in a black leather Legion uniform split across the battleground in a burst of inhuman speed, her pale blonde hair swooshing across her face as she slashed through the enemy ranks with her fire sword. She threw a look over her shoulder, and that's when I saw her face—*my* face—staring back at me.

She sprang into the air, then slammed her fist down. Jets of fire erupted from the ground, shooting up into raging pillars of flames. She strode across the battlefield, wings spreading out from her back, her dark purple-black feathers shimmering like petals of luxurious velvet in the light of the setting sun. Bodies fell before her. Men turned and ran from her. The ground shook beneath her.

A jolt of pain ruptured my ribcage. I looked down to find a sword protruding from my chest. I turned around to face the person who'd stabbed me in the back, but I blacked out before I could see their face.

I jumped up, ripped from that nightmare. The sounds of battle still echoed in my ears. Slowly, they faded away as consciousness found me. I looked around, but I didn't recognize where I was. I was in a bed not my own, covered in blankets that smelled of daisies and lemonade. This wasn't my room, and it definitely wasn't the Legion's medical ward.

I touched my neck. The skin was smooth, the wound completely healed. All of me was healed. I threw off the blankets and stood, but a wave of dizziness hit me, shoving me back into bed.

"Relax. Take it easy," Harker said. "Your body just healed some pretty severe injuries."

I looked across the dark room to find him sitting in the chair in the corner. "You healed me."

"Yes, you were in bad shape. If you hadn't tasted the gods' first gift, I wouldn't have been able to save you. That resilience was the difference between life and death."

I'd come so close to dying, to destroying any chance of saving Zane. So close. I had to get stronger.

"Thank you," I told Harker, getting to my feet more slowly this time.

He smiled. "You're welcome.

"But I'm still angry with you."

His smile faltered. "I had to tell the Legion where we were going. It's dangerous to go alone into a situation like that without backup. There's a reason this isn't standard procedure, and it's not because the Legion wants to annoy

Leda Pierce. And I'm glad they came and managed to fight through the vampires. Without their help, we would both be dead."

"You killed Rose," I shot back. "What happened to mercy? I know you didn't have to kill her."

"That *was* mercy. Punishment is slower. A lot slower."

I'd heard about the Legion's punishments, but I'd never seen them myself. I was pretty sure I didn't want to.

I sighed. Harker was loyal to the Legion through and through. I should have known better than to bring him along. And now, because of my decision, Rose was dead. What was I going to tell Ivy? Sure, maybe Rose would have died anyway. She wasn't exactly playing safely with fire. But if I hadn't acted as I had, she wouldn't have died because of me. I wasn't sure Ivy would forgive me. How could she when I didn't even forgive myself?

I looked around, noticing that big canopy over the bed for the first time. I was in Harker's apartment. In his bed. And I was wearing shorts and a tank top, not my uniform.

"Why am I wearing these clothes?" I asked him.

"Your uniform was cut through and drenched in your own blood."

I blushed.

"I was a perfect gentleman, I assure you. I asked Bianca to change you."

"And why am I here instead of in the medical ward?" I asked.

"After that last battle, the medical ward is full. You healed faster than the others. Faster than you should have been able to." He gave me a funny look, one I couldn't quite decipher. Either he was intrigued or appalled. In either case…

"I should be going," I told him.

He caught my hand as I passed by, turning me to face him. "I really like you, Leda." His voice dipped lower, and a small smile twisted his lips. Intrigued it was then.

"Ok…"

That was my eloquent response. Truth be told, I didn't know what to say to him. I liked him too, but he was just so…perfect. He didn't break the rules, not ever. That's why he'd told the Legion about our little scouting mission tonight. He just couldn't help himself. He was a good boy.

But I wasn't a good girl. I was going to break the rules and lots of them to save my brother from the gods and demons and whoever else might want to use him for their own gain. I didn't think Harker would be ok with that. In fact, I *knew* he wouldn't be ok with that. My utter disregard for authority went against everything the Legion of Angels, hand of the gods' will, stood for. Everything Harker Locke stood for.

So his next words nearly stunned me to silence.

"Do you want to save your brother?" he asked.

I knew he'd remember that. "Yes," I said cautiously.

"I can help you."

I blinked in surprise. "How?"

"With this." He pulled a glass vial from his jacket, setting it in my hands. It was filled with a sparkling fluid—blinding white, shining like liquid diamonds.

"What is it?" I asked.

"A one-way ticket to level nine."

"Ghost's Whisper," I whispered.

"Yes."

"Where did you get it?"

Confusion crinkled his brow. "What?"

"I'm pretty sure the gods don't leave that stuff just lying around."

"No, it's heavily guarded. But I have a friend."

I sighed. "Please don't tell me you stole from the gods."

"Ok, I won't tell you that." He grinned at me. "It's for you. I got it for you, Leda."

I'd been so wrong about him. He was as wicked as I was, trouble in so many ways. I looked down at that tiny vial of sparkling fluid.

"What are you waiting for?" he asked. "Isn't this exactly what you wanted? This is how you will save your brother."

He was right, but standing here, staring down at that magic in a bottle, I couldn't help but hesitate. Drinking this would make me an angel. It would give me powers I'd only ever dreamed of, but it would also change me. Irrevocably. Was I ready for it?

Yes, I decided, thinking of Zane. I would change for him, to save him. I *had* to change to save him. With that decided, I uncorked the vial. I was about to drink it down when a rush of magic cut through the room, carrying Nero inside. His sword was drawn and flaming, his wings spread wide. His gaze flickered to the vial in my hand before meeting my eyes again.

"Leda, I can't let you drink that."

CHAPTER TWENTY-ONE
Secret

"NERO," I SAID, struggling to keep my words civil. "I don't need another lecture about proper procedures."

"You can't drink that," he replied, undeterred by my icy tone. "If you do, it will kill you. It's the gods' Nectar, concentrated. It's the most potent stuff they have. It's what the gods themselves drink. It won't just make you an angel, it will essentially make you a god."

"And?"

"And within the week, it will kill you," he added definitively.

I glanced over at Harker, whose mouth thinned into a stubborn line. But beyond that stubbornness lay a hint of something else: guilt.

"So it's true," I said.

"The Nectar of the gods is pure magic," replied Harker. "What we soldiers of the Legion drink in the ceremonies is only a diluted version of the real thing. The first dose has only a drop of the Nectar. With each successive level, the dose is more potent. Until you get to this." He pointed at the vial.

Nero gave him a hard look. "Only an angel of the

highest level can drink this and survive."

"Why would you give this to me?" I asked Harker.

He didn't answer.

Nero answered for him. "Because he was told to."

"What do you mean?"

"Harker has been taking his orders from a god," said Nero. "Earlier today, I followed whispers of a plot to kill you. Only I didn't find what I expected. This god doesn't want to kill you. He wants to use you to find your brother. A telepath." He paused. "That is your secret."

Now I was the one not talking.

Nero's eyes slid over to Harker, his voice dropping to dangerous levels. "You like her. *Really* like her. I know you do. And you are trading her for your wings."

I swallowed the taste of betrayal, and it burned the whole way down. "You were promised wings?" I asked Harker. I couldn't even look at him.

"I was."

"How long?" I growled. "How long were you playing me?"

"It wasn't like that, Leda. I do like you."

I wasn't interested in platitudes, only answers. "How long?"

"Since you joined."

"That's why you were helping me," I realized, laughing bitterly. "You needed to get me strong enough."

"You needed the gods' first gift before you could take this without dying instantly." His gaze flickered to the vial in my hands. "But I don't think you'd die in a week."

"A month then?" I snapped.

"Isn't that what you were willing to do, to risk your life to save your brother?" he asked. "And, for the record, drinking the Nectar wouldn't have killed you."

I couldn't guess if he really believed those words. And I wouldn't try to. Apparently, I had the worst lie detector on the planet.

But Nero sure wasn't buying it. "That Nectar kills anyone below level ten," he told Harker. "It would kill me."

"You didn't see how fast she healed, Nero. And remember how she took right to the second dose of Nectar. There's something about her. She's different. My god told me as much. He guaranteed me that she wouldn't die."

"You used me." I hurled the words in his face and hoped they hurt him more than they hurt me. I was petty that way. "You pretended to care about me."

"I didn't pretend."

"You used me for your own personal gain. I will not help you enslave my brother."

With that said, I threw the vial to the floor. The glass shattered, and the fluid spilled out, quickly losing its shimmer.

"It is the will of the gods," Harker told me. "There's no way around it."

"It is not the will of the gods. It is the will of one god, a play he's making," Nero said.

"Do you know which god?" I asked him.

"No." That appeared to annoy him to no end. "But I will find out and then report this to the Council of Gods."

"You have no idea who you're messing with," Harker told us.

"No. You don't know who *you* are messing with." I punched him in the face.

It was a good punch, fast, crisp, powerful—but it never would have gotten through Harker's defenses if he hadn't been gazing wistfully at the liquid evaporating at my feet. As Harker straightened to fight back, Nero shot him with a tranquilizer much bigger than the ones we'd used on the vampires. Harker took a single, staggered step forward, then collapsed unconscious to the floor.

"I had it," I told Nero as he bound Harker's hands and feet.

"No offense, Pandora, but one lucky punch does not make you ready to take on a seventh level soldier of the Legion."

"He's still weak from the last fight," I pointed out.

"And so are you."

"I don't like the way you argue."

He arched a single eyebrow at me. "With logic?"

"Exactly."

He gave me a funny look.

"What?"

"Harker was right about you," he said. "You are different. Special. There's an energy about you. I can't explain it."

There wasn't anything to explain—or anything special about me, just my stubborn will to save my brother and to protect those I loved.

"What are you going to do?" I asked quietly. "About me?"

"You mean, am I going to report you and tell the Legion what your brother is?"

I nodded mutely.

"Obviously you don't know me very well."

I looked down at Harker. "I didn't know him very well."

"I am not Harker," Nero said, setting his hands on my shoulders. "I told you everyone joins the Legion for a reason. His was power. And the need for order. He wanted to be an angel. And he couldn't say no to a god's command."

"And you?"

Nero grunted. "I already am an angel. And I say no to commands far too often for my own good. Your secret is safe with me."

"Thank you." I set my hands over his, squeezing them in appreciation. "I don't know how long this will last. One of the gods already knows about Zane. How long before he tells the others?"

"He won't. The gods play their power games with one another as much as they do with the demons. They are always trying to get the upper hand over the others. This god, whoever he is, obviously wants to use your brother as a weapon, to strengthen his position against the others."

"How do you know?" I asked.

"Because if all the gods knew, they would already be looking for your brother. And you wouldn't be standing here."

"I'd be tied up, being tortured for information."

"Yes."

I laughed. It was a hard laugh, full of sorrow and desperation. Not that I was taken aback by his bluntness. I guess I'd gotten used to it. I'd even started to appreciate it. Not that I was going to admit that to Nero. There was no need to issue him an open invitation to torture me.

"If the gods don't have Zane—and the demons don't have him—then who does?" I asked Nero.

"I don't know," he said, frowning. "But we are going to find out."

CHAPTER TWENTY-TWO
The Promise

WHILE NERO BROUGHT Harker to wherever misbehaving soldiers of the Legion ended up, I went back to my dormitory to check on Ivy. She was sitting with Drake on her bed, but she jumped up as soon as I entered the room.

"I heard you nearly got killed. I'm so glad you're all right." She hugged me. "What happened?"

I sat down on her bed, patting the mattress to invite her to do the same. Then I told her and Drake about what had happened with Rose and the vampires tonight. Ivy cried, then fumed, then she cried some more. Finally, she threw her arms around me and hugged me like a sister.

"I'm sorry," I said, my eyes wet, my mouth dry. "I shouldn't have brought Harker there. This is my fault."

"I don't blame you for my mother's death." Her eyes narrowed. "I blame him. I know that's stupid. She was spearheading a revolution against the gods. She did terrible things. And yet…"

"You still love her," I said.

"Yeah. I do." She hugged her knees and rocked back and forth. "Isn't that crazy?"

"Love is crazy. It's not rational at all."

"Yeah." She wiped the back of her hand across her eyes. "Speaking of me being irrational, where is that Harker? I know he was just doing his job, but I really need to go kick his ass."

"He says he killed her out of mercy. He says they would have tortured her."

Ivy sniffled.

"And Harker isn't here," I said quietly.

Drake met my eyes. "What happened?"

"Nero is bringing him before the High Angels."

"For killing my mother?" Ivy asked, blinking in confusion.

"No, for giving me a vial of pure Nectar."

"The food of the gods," Drake gasped. "Where did he get it?"

"And why did he give it to you?" Ivy asked.

"It's a long story," I said.

She took my hand. "I love long stories."

"Especially with happy endings," Drake added, taking my other hand.

"The ending remains to be seen," I said, then looked toward the door.

A gentle tug at the periphery of my senses had told me Nero was standing in our open doorway, and there he was. If only that little trick could always work, then he'd never be able to sneak up on me.

"Leda," he said.

"This must be serious if he's not calling me Pandora," I told my friends.

The statement clearly didn't amuse Nero as much as it had them. His face remained inscrutable. "I wish to speak to you."

I glanced at Ivy.

"Go," she said, waving me away.

"Are you sure?"

Her eyes flickered to Drake, and I understood. She wanted to be alone with him, to let him comfort her. So I got up and followed Nero into the hall. We walked side-by-side in silence until we reached his apartment. Even larger than Harker's, its white marble floors shone like ice. A large leather sofa sat opposite a television that covered most of the wall. It was all very nice, very posh even—but none of it felt lived in. This might have been where he slept, but it wasn't his home. I wondered where that special place was for him.

"So, when I'm an angel, will I get such an awesome place?" I asked.

"I'm sure it will be much better."

I jumped at the brush of his words against my ear, so close that each syllable caressed my skin. I hadn't heard him approach. Those angels were way too quiet. We stared at each other for a few moments, the angel and I. The silence was positively deafening. I wished I knew what he was thinking.

"How did it go with Harker?" I asked him, just to break the silence.

"I brought him to the High Angels. What they do with him remains to be seen."

The silence returned with a vengeance, stretching on to eternity.

"Your plan is insane," he finally said.

"Oh?"

"Yes. What made you think you could simply join the Legion of Angels and jump up to the ninth level just like that?"

"Dogged determination," I told him with a smile.

The angel remained unimpressed.

"Ok, I didn't think it would be just like that," I said. "I knew it would be difficult."

"What you've faced so far is nothing compared to what is to come, to the horrors you will face. You will be tested in ways you cannot begin to imagine."

"If you're trying to scare me—"

"I'm trying to *help* you," he told me.

I thought about that for a moment, and it just didn't make sense. "Why?"

"Because Harker was right about one thing. You are different. There's something about you." He stared me straight in the eye and didn't even blink. "You will have an important role to play in this world, Leda Pierce. I can feel it."

I shrugged. "I'm just a girl from Purgatory."

"Not anymore," he told me, his hand brushing across my jaw. "Now, you are a soldier in the Legion of Angels. And you will make it to the ninth level. I will make sure of it. This I promise you."

"Nero…I don't know what to say. Thank you."

"You can thank me by letting me help you, instead of going off after vampires and gods know what else and trying to do it all by yourself, thinking that will protect everyone else. Promise me now that you won't do that again. You nearly died, Leda."

"I didn't know you cared," I said with a coy smile.

"I will train you," he said, immune to my charms. Or maybe I wasn't nearly as charming as I thought I was. "I will help you get through the levels."

No one had ever made it through the levels of the Legion faster than Nero. I couldn't have asked for a better coach.

"I will be tough on you," he warned me.

"Oh, I never would have guessed. You've been so easy on me up to this point." I smirked at him.

"You might hate me by the end of it."

"I can live with that."

He snorted. "There's one more thing. Something we can try if you wish."

His gaze dipped to my lips briefly before it jerked back up to my eyes. I was suddenly and totally aware of how close he was standing to me. I didn't answer him, uncertain if this was his way of propositioning me. And what I would say if he was.

"I can help you see your brother," he told me. Whatever next words I'd expected, those weren't it.

"What?"

"Just for a second," he clarified. "I can connect to him."

"But I thought that the better you know someone, the more easily you can link to them. You don't know my brother at all."

"No, but I do know *you*. I can use your connection to your brother to find him." He paused. "If we exchange blood."

The last time I'd drunk his blood, I had been so crazed with lust than I'd nearly jumped him in the club's hallway. I hadn't been able to think straight. All I'd wanted was him. Things had been hardly better when he'd drunk from me. Whatever was between us, if I gave into it, it was going to drive me mad. But if it would help me figure out where Zane was, it was worth the risk.

"Let's do it," I told him.

◆ ◇ ◆ ◇ ◆

Nero pulled the curtains closed and dimmed the lights in his apartment. Then he pulled fifty candles out of a gigantic box and set them up all around the living room. They looked pretty and smelled better: like vanilla and strawberries and peaches. Nero waved his hand, and the flames flickered to life on all the candles at once.

He extended his hand to me, motioning me forward. Swallowing my doubt, burying it beneath a mountain of resolve, I walked up to him and took his hand. He took my other hand too, his hold firm but not rough. Slow and smooth, he lowered into his knees, and I followed the motion of his body, lowering with him.

He met my eyes. "Are you ready?"

I nodded.

He released one of my hands and drew the knife strapped to his thigh. He pricked his finger with the tip. As blood beaded on the surface of his skin, heat flooded me, a wave of fire washing from my head to my tiptoes. My mouth ached—no, my whole body ached. Ached for his blood. For him. I felt my fangs descending, searing my gums with savage need.

"Sorry," I said, pressing my lips together. My back arched forward, pushing out my breasts. My hips rocked toward him, opening. I realized what I was doing and pulled back. "Sorry."

He caught my retreating hand. "Don't be sorry."

"I have to learn to control this."

"You will."

"When?"

He chuckled, and I realized I had my hand on his thigh. I dropped it hastily.

"A few months," he said. "Your body is still getting accustomed to the new magic raging through it."

There was something more than magic raging through my body. Hormones. Raw, savage hormones that were telling me to throw that gorgeous angel to the ground and have my way with him right here and now.

I felt a cool breeze on my chest, and I realized I'd pulled off my shirt and tossed it aside. And even though I knew I should have been embarrassed, all I could think about was that I was still wearing too much clothing. And so was he.

"What is wrong with me?" I asked him, clenching my teeth against the raging desire inside of me.

"You're just more sensitive to magic than most people."

And sensitive to him. Why him?

He flicked the tip of his knife, pricking my finger too. Blood surged to the surface like a swimmer gasping for air. I pushed my hand into his face, demanding that he drink from me.

"Steady," he said. "Just a drop each. That's all we need to perform the spell."

I didn't care about that damned spell. And only one drop? Screw that. I wanted to bathe in the glorious ecstasy of his blood, to relish in the euphoria of his magic melting into mine.

His grip tightened around my wrists, holding back my grasping hands. "Leda, you are stronger than this."

No, I wasn't. Not when it came to his blood. It tasted like Nectar. A little drop of heaven. Something about it made me lose my mind.

"Think about your brother. About Zane."

The sound of my brother's name on his lips drew me out of my madness. I took a deep breath, blocking out the pounding, aching pulse in my veins. I cleared my throat and looked at Nero's finger, counting back from ten. On one, I dipped my head very slowly to his hand, showing him that I was in control. My tongue darted out and licked the drop of blood from his finger.

I stood very still, even as a tidal wave of need crashed through me, setting every nerve in my body on fire. I gasped, quivering, resisting. Nero watched me with intense curiosity, his gaze boring into mine even as his tongue flicked out and licked the drop of blood from my finger.

I sensed a change in him immediately. He grew oddly still, like he was struggling every bit as much as I was. His eyes lit up, glowing with magic. His mouth softened, his lips parting. Slowly, languidly, his tongue slipped out to trace the inside of his lower lip.

It took every shred of willpower in me not to pounce on him. Willpower was in short supply here. I could see Nero struggling to retain his composure. His hands shook as he extended them out to me, palms up. As I set my hands on his, a burst of something I'd never felt before surged through me. It was as cold as a whispering winter's night, and it was that breath of ice that froze the desire right out of me.

Bright blurs of light danced before my eyes. Snowflakes. I blinked down hard a few times. No, not snowflakes. Dandelion seeds. Millions and millions of them dancing on a warm summer breeze. Beneath the dandelion sky, children held hands and danced in circles across a grassy field, barefoot and free. There were no buildings, no wall, no black prairies or rotting forests—nothing but pristine nature in sight for miles and miles. The children's laughter melted the ice from my skin. The frosty particles rose in the wind like shards of broken glass, dissolving into the sky.

The sun flashed, and then I was standing in a room lit

up by a ceiling of sparkling magic lanterns. And Zane stood before me, holding out his hands to me, a smile on his face. I tried to call out his name, but the words wouldn't leave my mouth. Everything around me began to unravel, the streamers of its existence slithering away as the magic of the spell faded, hurling me out of this vision.

I jumped to my feet in Nero's apartment, adrenaline raging in my veins, desperation fueling my steps. I needed to get to Zane, but I didn't know where to go, so I channeled the energy into pacing back and forth across the floor.

"Did you see?" I asked Nero as he rose to his feet. "Did you see him?"

"Yes."

"That place. Such beautiful, peaceful nature, untouched by monsters. There's no place on Earth like it. We have only scorched expanses of nothingness—and cities built past the walls we hide behind. What is that place we saw? Where is my brother?"

"I don't know. It is not any place I know of."

"He looked happy," I said. "I think…well, I just have this feeling that he's safe there, wherever *there* is. At least for now. But I have to find out where he is. I have to see him, to know for myself. To talk to him."

"Leda."

I kept pacing, faster and faster. "I had a dream earlier. A battlefield of death. Or maybe it was something else. I don't know. I feel like something is happening here. Something beyond us." I laughed. "Listen to me, going on about dreams and doomsday premonitions. Am I going crazy? Is this what madness feels like?"

Nero reached out and grabbed my hand. "Leda."

I pivoted around to face him. "I need to find Zane."

"And you will," he said. "I promised I would help you, didn't I?"

"Yes, but—"

"No buts," he told me. "You need to calm down. For the moment, your brother is not in danger. You need to focus on what's important."

"Gaining the magic I need to find him," I said.

"Exactly. This is the path you have chosen, the path you were meant to take," he said. "Your new training starts now. You must push yourself harder than ever before."

He took two swords off of his wall. "I will not relent." He handed one of the swords to me. "And neither can you."

"I won't," I promised, holding to my weapon.

"Good." He raised his sword. "Then let's see what you've got."

Author's Note

If you want to be notified when I have a new release, head on over to my website to sign up for my mailing list at http://www.ellasummers.com/newsletter. Your e-mail address will never be shared, and you can unsubscribe at any time.

If you enjoyed *Vampire's Kiss*, I'd really appreciate if you could spread the word. One of the best ways of doing that is by leaving a review wherever you purchased this book. Thank you for your invaluable support!

Witch's Cauldron, the second book in the *Legion of Angels* series, is now available.

About the Author

Ella Summers has been writing stories for as long as she could read; she's been coming up with tall tales even longer than that. One of her early year masterpieces was a story about a pigtailed princess and her dragon sidekick. Nowadays, she still writes fantasy. She likes books with lots of action, adventure, and romance. When she is not busy writing or spending time with her two young children, she makes the world safe by fighting robots.

Ella is the international bestselling author of the paranormal and fantasy series *Legion of Angels*, *Dragon Born*, and *Sorcery and Science*.

www.ellasummers.com

Printed in Great Britain
by Amazon